THE BEAT

Asking For It

Something's wrong. A single glance tells the thief that this isn't a guy's room, it's a girl's room. There are clothes, cassettes, books and stuff scattered across the floor. The thief realizes that he's made a mistake, that he ought to leave the room quickly, before...

Then he hears a whimpering sound, coming from the side of the bed. Common sense tells him to get out of the room this moment. A smaller, but more insistent voice tells him to stay.

"Are you all right?" he calls, softly, before taking a step forward, looking.

On the floor, a naked girl with short hair pulls a towel around her bruised body.

"Help me," she says.

This novel does not include graphic sexual violence. However, because of its subject matter, some readers may find certain scenes disturbing.

Other titles by David Belbin in the Point Crime series:

Coming soon in Point Crime:

POINT CRIME

THE BEAT

Asking For It

David Belbin

SCHOLASTIC

The city in these pages is real. The events described in them are not. All of the characters, together with the police station where some of them work, are imaginary. The author wishes to thank the many people, including serving police officers, who helped him with this series. He alone is responsible for any mistakes.

Scholastic Children's Books
Commonwealth House, 1–19 New Oxford Street,
London WC1A 1NU, UK
a division of Scholastic Ltd
London ~ New York ~ Toronto ~ Sydney ~ Auckland

First published in the UK by Scholastic Ltd, 1996

Copyright © David Belbin, 1996

ISBN 0 590 13369 1

Typeset by TW Typesetting, Midsomer Norton, Avon

Printed by Cox & Wyman Ltd, Reading, Berks.

10 9 8 7 6 5 4 3 2 1

PROLOGUE

Some people invite you to burgle them. Some still leave doors and windows open. Others have locks which can be opened with a credit card in less time than it takes to pick a pocket. Failing that, some have doors which collapse with the first kick. They have ground-floor windows which cannot be seen from the street. Their neighbours make so much noise, they wouldn't hear a bomb going off, unless it happened in their living-room. Yes, some people are asking to be burgled.

The thief doesn't accept every invitation. Being lazy, he only goes for places where the pickings are easy, the risks minimal. Once, he went after the usual: videos, TVs, hi-fis. But these items are bulky and conspicuous, therefore dangerous. Nowadays, he prefers to take things which fit snugly into his shoulder bag: CDs, watches, cameras, calculators. Best of all: cheque books, cheque cards, credit cards. Ideally: cash.

Where to steal from? The richest pickings used to be from the prosperous middle classes. But now they've got burglar alarms and neighbourhood watch schemes. They're best left to the professionals, who can be in and out in a minute, taking a baseball bat to anyone who gets in their way.

The children of the middle classes, however, are a different story. They have all the consumer goods, but none of the security. They're so casual about their possessions, you'd think they wanted to be burgled. It gives them something to talk about with their friends, one more reason to complain about the world.

The thief wanders around a university hall of residence on a Friday afternoon in early May. This hall has been good to him before, so he's hopeful. His usual technique is to show up in the morning, slipping into rooms just after their occupants have gone off to lectures. It's easy to tell which rooms are empty because the pigeon-holes in the foyer will be empty, too. Friday afternoons aren't so good. The place is nice and quiet. Plenty of people are out. Some of them have gone away for the weekend. Sadly, they've taken their wallets and purses with them. All the thief's picked up so far are a bunch of indie CDs, an Olympus AF10 and a CD Walkman with portable speakers.

The stuff in his bag will bring in forty, maybe fifty pounds. But the thief wants more. He wants enough money to have a really good weekend. So he climbs another set of stairs, walks stealthily down another corridor, looking for one more room with "burgle me" scrawled on its welcome mat. With each set of stairs, there's more risk – he has further to run if challenged. The first rule of burglary is this: have a safe escape route planned, and he has. Each floor has a fire door – not alarmed – which can be opened from the inside, but not out.

The room he's going to try next had nothing in its pigeon-hole. The thief knocks on the door. No reply. There's a decent sized gap between the door and its side post. The thief pulls a Visa card from his jeans pocket, pushes it into the gap so that the spring bolt is pushed back. He presses the door, wiggles the credit card and – *hey presto!* – he's in.

The room is practically empty. There's a bunch of textbooks on the shelf, some notes on the desk. There's a poster saying *Jesus Saves* above it. The thief looks under the bed. He goes through the desk. The most exciting thing in it is a pack of condoms. He looks behind the books. Finally, he pulls out the Bible, holding it open with his gloved hands so that any enclosures flutter to the ground.

Out falls a shiny, plastic credit card. A broad smile fills the thief's face.

The name on the card is male, which is useful. The thief can learn to copy the signature, then use it himself, rather than selling it on for a pittance. The way it's hidden suggests that the credit card's owner has been keeping it for emergencies. He'll have been cautious about using it, even though the credit limit will only be five or six hundred pounds. The thief will be cautious, too. He intends to get full value out of this card.

The thief tidies up quickly. If he leaves the room as he finds it, then, hopefully, it will be a few days before the victim notices that the card's gone. Maybe he won't find out until he suddenly gets a huge bill.

Satisfied that the room is straight, the thief checks that the corridor is clear, then slips out. He intends to leave the building, dump his takings in a safe place, then shoot into town for a spending spree on the credit card.

The thief reckons without the guy who charges out of his room on the floor below, barging into him as he passes, knocking the bag from his shoulder to the floor. The guy trots down the stairs without an apology. The thief watches the guy go, clocking his ugly, arrogant face. The guy doesn't look back at the thief, which is good. Then the thief looks at the door through which the guy has just come. It's ajar.

If ever a guy was asking for it, it's this one. The thief picks up his bag and nudges the door open. He can still feel the throb in his shoulder from where the guy knocked against him. He will enjoy...

Something's wrong. A single glance tells the thief that this isn't a guy's room, it's a girl's room. In fact, the thief remembers, all the rooms on this floor are for women. And this one's a mess. There are clothes, cassettes, books and stuff scattered across the floor. The bed is made, yet there's the unmistakable smell of sex. The thief realizes that he's made a mistake, that he ought to leave the room quickly, before...

Then he hears a whimpering sound, coming from the side of the bed. Common sense tells him to get out of the room this moment. A smaller, but more insistent voice tells him to stay.

"Are you all right?" he calls, softly, before taking a step forward, looking.

On the floor, a naked girl with short hair pulls a towel around her bruised body.

"Help me," she says.

1

It was a warm afternoon, far too hot for the time of year. Lorraine's lecture finished early, which was a good thing, because she'd nearly fallen asleep towards the end. She walked back to hall, her body sticky and in need of a shower. Before going to her room, though, she decided to call in on Sophie, who ought to have been in the lecture, too. They usually walked back together. Maybe Sophie had gone home early for the weekend, but it didn't do any harm to check.

Lorraine knocked on the third-floor door but there was no reply. She knocked again and was about to go when a feeble voice called out:

"Who is it?"

"Me. Lorraine."

"Hold on."

Lorraine waited while a shuffling sound approached the door. Sophie opened the door part way, on the chain, which she never normally used, then let Lorraine in.

"What's happened?" Lorraine asked. "You look awful."

Sophie got back into bed. "Sick," was all she said.

"Can I get you anything? Have you been to the doctor?"

Sophie shook her head to both questions.

"Just want to stay here."

Lorraine frowned. "Do you want to borrow my notes from the lecture?"

"Next week, maybe," Sophie said, slowly. "I think I'm going to go home for a few days."

"OK. Fine. I'll look in on you later, all right?"

"All right, thanks."

Lorraine walked along the corridor thinking about Sophie. She had never seen her looking that way before. Her face was pale and puffy, but she didn't look ill. She looked frightened.

What happened next, however, drove thoughts of Sophie from Lorraine's mind. For, when she opened the door to her room, everything she owned was scattered across the floor. No, she realized, after she'd taken a few breaths and had a closer look: not quite everything.

She'd been burgled.

*　*　*

Uniformed coppers called CID officers "nine to fivers". It was an insult, not an accurate description. Today, for instance, Neil Foster's shift was on a three to eleven and, though it was Friday, the weekend seemed a long way off. The sergeant took a phone call, then turned to Neil.

"I think we can let you handle this one on your own, mate," Chris Dylan said, with a smile which told the young officer he wasn't doing him a favour.

"What?"

"Burglary at Wordsworth Hall, student residence for Trent University."

"I know where it is," Neil said, "but why are we going out? I thought the uniforms dealt with all the petty thefts these days?"

Dylan gave Neil a sarcastic smile. "Normally, yes. But there've been two burglaries this afternoon, which takes the total up to nine this term. That's three a week. They may only be students, but I think they deserve some protection. Don't you?"

"I guess so."

"Cast your eyes over this before you go."

Neil read the file. He had only been on CID for a few weeks, yet already he found himself amazed by how plod-like the behaviour of his uniformed colleagues could be. There had been seven break-ins (more, probably, because uninsured students were unlikely to report small thefts), but the notes revealed no hard evidence about the thief's *modus operandi*. The reports were so casual, you got the impression that the burglar had simply walked into an unlocked room, taken what he wanted, and left.

Burglary was brutally common. The police couldn't pretend to investigate every case. When the value of items stolen was small, as in these instances, CID would not be called in. There would be no fingerprinting, no investigation of any sort, only a few words about home security from a beat copper and a leaflet from Victim Support.

Neil got to the hall of residence just before nine, three and a half hours after the initial report. This wasn't bad going for CID, but he wasn't surprised to find that the victim who'd called the police, Lorraine Parker, was fed up about having been kept waiting for ages.

"I haven't eaten, you know. I was meant to be meeting some friends an hour ago."

"I'll try and make it as quick as possible," Neil told her. "What's missing?"

Lorraine told him. She hadn't lost much – a CD Walkman, some speakers and a couple of dozen CDs.

"Oh, and some money."

"How much?"

"Fifty, sixty quid. It was money I had for the weekend."

"Are you insured?"

"I think so. On my parents' policy. I'll have to check with them."

Neil wrote all this down. He didn't believe her about the money. Most people exaggerated when it came to insurance claims and cash was the one thing which was impossible to prove. You might eventually recover stolen hi-fi equipment which turned out to be nowhere near as expensive as the owner claimed, but who kept a note of the serial numbers on their banknotes? It was a foolproof crime. The victims saw the bit extra as their way of getting compensation for the trauma of being burgled. If they really had been burgled.

"There's no sign of forced entry," Neil pointed out.

Lorraine agreed. "The door was locked as normal when I got back. But it's pretty easy for people to get in downstairs. They just have to press the buzzer, pretend to be visiting someone and go up."

This was possible, Neil thought, but most burglars would hate someone being able to identify them.

"I noticed that each floor has a door to the fire escape," he said. "Is it possible to get in through them?"

"Not unless someone's not shut them properly. They only open from the inside."

Neil examined the lock on Lorraine's door. It was child's play. He could send out for fingerprints, but it was pointless. There wouldn't be any. He gave

Lorraine a crime number and asked her to give him a ring if she heard or remembered anything.

The other victim was also on floor C. Actually, it was possible that there was more than one other victim, but the victim didn't know it yet. On his previous visit, the thief had twice hit two rooms, but the time before, he did three (presuming that all the burglaries had been reported).

Melanie Byatt was a looker. She had long brown hair and a slim, shapely body. She seemed like a nice person, too. Unlike Lorraine, she showed no irritation about being kept waiting.

"It's late," she said, after making Neil a coffee in the floor's communal kitchen. "Are you on over-time?"

"No. My shift doesn't finish until eleven."

"There's not much to report," Melanie told him. "All he got was my camera."

"Do you have a serial number for it?"

She shook her head. "If there was one, I don't know it."

"I'm surprised he took so little."

"Not much to take. This is the second time I've been done this term."

"Ah, I'm sorry." Neil should have checked the notes more carefully. "Are you insured?" he asked.

"For what it's worth. My excess is £75. The camera wasn't worth much more than that."

"What did they take last time?"

"My stereo. My CD collection. Did you know that insurance companies will only insure students for a maximum of £100 worth of CDs? I had ten times that many."

"I'm sorry."

Melanie shrugged. "I should never have brought them with me. Now I use cassettes and a crappy old tape player which no one in their right mind would want to steal. You learn from your mistakes."

"Any cash taken?" Neil asked, softly, expecting her to take the hint and make something up.

"No." Melanie smiled. She had a toothy, goofy smile which said she knew exactly what he was getting at. "They don't insure cash, either," she explained.

"Well, if you think of anything, I'll be around for an hour or so, asking questions... I'll try to see the warden about getting a new lock put on your door. They should have done that last time you were burgled. This one's a cinch."

"Now you tell me," Melanie said, with a wry smile.

"Thanks for the coffee."

Neil saw himself out, then began knocking on the doors. The hall had four floors. Women occupied the first and third floors, men the other two. The burglar never touched the first floor, presumably because the warden had an office at the end of it. Neil started with the third floor, since both of today's burglaries had taken place there. Only one other person was in. A pale girl with short hair was leaving her room with a large bag. She flinched before Neil identified himself.

"I only need a minute of your time. There was an intruder in the hall this afternoon. I wondered, were you in your room?"

"Yes."

"All afternoon?"

"Yes."

"Did you see or hear anything?"

"No."

"Nothing at all?"

The girl had spoken without looking at him.

"OK. If you could just tell me your name so that I don't bother you again."

"Sophie Turner."

"Off home for the weekend?"

"For a few days, yes."

"Sorry to have bothered you."

That girl looks disturbed about something, Neil thought, as he watched her walk slowly down the stairs. But he had more important things to think about.

Ruth Clarke and Clare Coppola walked into the Peacock at half past nine. It only took a second to locate Clare's shift in the left-hand corner of the bar. Unnoticed, Clare listened to their conversation while Ruth bought the drinks. Gary, who was to join the shift a week on Monday, was asking about the shift sergeant.

"Jan Hunt," John Farraday was saying. "Not everyone likes her at first. Sour-faced cow, that's what our old sergeant used to call her, when she wasn't around. But she's got his job now. And, actually, she grows on you. Mind you, Jan probably won't be around for long. Got a young kid, Henry. She'll be having another soon and leaving the force, mark my words."

"And the inspector," Gary was asking. "What's he like?"

"A high flyer," Ben Shipman said. "He's on the graduate fast track scheme. Youngest inspector in the county."

"Yeah, but, what's he like?"

"Efficient. Fair. Keeps himself to himself."

"He won't be out with us tonight, then?"

"Doubt it," Tim Cooper said, in a somewhat smug voice. "Not really his scene. If you ask me, he's…"

Tim whispered something in Gary's ear. Clare could guess what it was. She didn't like Tim Cooper much. Not that she saw a lot of him. They had never been partnered and he was off sick a lot.

"Shove up, boys," Ruth said, putting down their drinks and adopting her life and soul of the party persona. "Make room for the glamour girls."

Ruth sat next to Ben, at the edge of the group.

14

Ruth wasn't on this shift. In fact, she worked at a different station. Ruth was based at South, while Clare worked at East. But Ruth, as well as being Clare's best friend, was going out with Ben, so she was welcome along. Clare would have preferred to sit with Ruth, but found herself sandwiched between John and the new recruit.

"So," Gary said. "You and me are the babies of the shift."

"S'right," Clare agreed. "Anything you want to know?"

"You're usually partnered with the sarge, aren't you?"

Clare nodded.

"Isn't that a bit unusual, two women out together?"

"It's just the way it happened."

"You get on with her?"

"She's a good sergeant."

Clare was trying to be diplomatic. She and Jan would never be bosom buddies, but they had learnt to respect each other.

"Where are you from?" Clare asked, changing the subject.

"Far end of the county. Worksop. Lived there twenty-one years, so I fancied a change, you know. Try the big city."

"You did something between school and the job, then?"

"Worked at Dad's butcher's for five years. Good

living, but I didn't want to spend the rest of me life at it. How about you?"

Gary was a little older than her, Clare realized. She was still the youngest member of the shift.

"I did a year at university. Architecture. Dropped out."

"You're an intellectual, then," he teased her. "Or did you fail your exams?"

Clare ignored the question. She'd never failed an exam in her life, but didn't want to show off.

"And you live with that bloke who used to be on the shift, Foster?"

"Neil. I go out with him. We don't live together."

"I see."

What did he see? Gary gave Clare a boyish grin and she returned it with a weak smile. Their new recruit fancied himself, she decided. But Clare didn't fancy him. He had a big build, with red hair and the baby fat not quite gone from his cheeks. Clare preferred leaner, more sensitive-looking men.

"Sorry I'm late," a familiar voice called. "Hope you lot aren't too far ahead of me. Shall I get them in?"

Jan Hunt went for a round of drinks without asking what anyone wanted. She knew her shift's drinking habits. Two minutes later, she deposited three pints and a mineral water on the table.

"Driving, are you, sarge?" Gary asked.

"No, Kevin dropped me off. That's for the boss. He's at the bar."

Paul Grace walked over, leather jacket, designer label jeans, carrying the other four drinks. He deposited a pint of Stella in front of Gary, who looked almost as surprised to see him as the other constables did.

"Welcome aboard," Grace said, lifting his glass of Perrier as he spoke. "Here's to the new gang."

Neil finished at ten past eleven. He felt like a drink, but it was past last orders. Home was just round the corner. He could drive there in two minutes. He would drink a can, make a few notes, have an early night. It was football tomorrow. He was looking forward to that.

"We meet again."

Neil looked round to see Melanie Byatt in a long summer dress. She looked out of place in it, like a little girl dressing up.

"Any luck?" she asked.

Neil shook his head. "'Fraid not. Going some-where exciting?"

"Just a party."

"On your own?"

"Anything wrong with that?" The words were critical, but she said them in a light-hearted way, with a friendly smile.

"Walking alone late at night – it can be dangerous – that's all."

"It's not far."

"In that case," Neil said. "Let me give you a lift. Get in."

"Thanks."

She was right. The party wasn't far. There wasn't even time for a conversation beyond Melanie asking Neil where he lived and how long he'd been in CID.

"Have a nice time," Neil said, as they pulled up outside the door.

"You can come in with me if you want."

Neil was taken aback. "I … eh, I'm not dressed for it."

"It's OK. You don't look like a policeman. Do you dance?"

"Yes, I…"

She gave him a flirtatious smile. "So, are you coming or not?"

Neil realized, with a small shock, that she fancied him.

"I have a girlfriend," he announced, in a sober voice.

Melanie looked amused. "Don't flatter yourself. I'm not trying to get off with you. I'm trying to be friendly. You look like you could do with a bit of company. Coming?"

"I appreciate the offer," Neil told her, "but I'm dog-tired. Some other time."

"Maybe I'll hold you to that."

"Good night, Melanie."

"You remembered my name, I'm impressed. But you've got the advantage over me."

18

"Neil."

"Good night, Neil."

He watched her walk into the party and wondered what he was missing.

Busy talking, they all missed the last bus. Paul Grace was giving Gary, Clare and Jan Hunt a lift home. He'd offered Ruth one, too, but she was walking back with Ben.

"He seemed all right, your inspector," she told her boyfriend. "Clare always makes him sound like a robot."

"He's like that at work," Ben said. "I haven't known him come out for a drink before."

"Maybe he hasn't been asked before."

"I dunno," Ben said. "It's hard to trust a man who doesn't drink."

"Now you're being silly," Ruth told him. "You're practically teetotal yourself."

Ben squeezed her hand. Without discussing it, they were heading back to his place. A dark thought crossed Ruth's mind.

"When does Charlene get back?" she asked.

There had been a couple of times when she'd stayed overnight with Ben and accidentally answered the phone the next morning, only to find his ex (or maybe not-so-ex) girlfriend on the line. She didn't want it to happen again.

"Sometime soon," Ben said. "But it's taking her

longer to get over the fire than the doctors first thought."

Charlene Harris had been burned in a fire at her office three weeks before.

"I'll probably see her," Ben added. "We go back a long way. We can't stop being friends, just like that. And I worry about her, working for Jagger. But it's over, I promise."

Jagger was Charlene's boss, a local solicitor who Ben had good reason to loathe.

"All right?" Ben asked, slipping his hand out of Ruth's and putting his arm around her waist, so that they walked closely, but more slowly, together.

"All right," Ruth told him.

A police car jumped the traffic lights behind them and swept down the wide road, lights flashing and siren blaring. Ruth and Ben stopped for a moment, then walked more hurriedly down the hill. They were halfway home.

2

The atmosphere at Meadow Lane was desperate. It was the last home game of the season and County had already been relegated. Not only that, but they were bottom of their division. Sheffield United, County's opponents, were just outside the play-off zone and had no chance of being promoted. Neil had been trying to get Clare along to a game all season, but she had agreed to come only now, when the result of the match was meaningless.

Still, it was good to have her here, on what used to be the terraces. It was a hot, May afternoon, more suitable for cricket than football. Neil hoped that this would be the first of many football matches they'd attend together. He used to be a season ticket holder, but now worked so many Saturdays that it would be a waste of money. Not that there was ever any trouble getting in. Across the Trent, every Forest game was a sell-out. These days, County's gate never got into five figures.

It was one of Neil's dreams: coming to County ever other weekend with his wife, and, in time, his kids, too. His dream might be on the verge of coming true, because Neil had finally worked up the nerve to ask Clare to marry him.

For days before then, he'd been anticipating Clare's reaction when he got down on his knees and said the words. After he did it, Clare didn't frown, or laugh, or rush out of the room. What she did was pull him back on to the sofa, and kiss him for a long, long time.

"Was that a 'yes' or a 'no'?" he asked, afterwards.

"It was a definite 'maybe'," Clare said, beaming a huge smile at him. "Can I have some time to think about it?"

"Take as much time as you like," Neil said.

So far, she had taken two weeks. Maybe, tonight, she would announce her decision. Maybe her coming to the match this afternoon was a good omen. But it wasn't a good game. There was no sniff of a goal. Even Neil, fanatic follower, was bored.

"Total football," someone called out, taking the michael, just as the whistle blew for half-time.

"Total rubbish," another voice called.

Clare looked at Neil strangely and he realized that the second voice had been his own.

"Come on," he said, "the meat pies here were once voted the best at a British ground."

"Who by?" she asked. "*Egon Ronay* or *The Good Food Guide*?"

But she did seem to enjoy the pie.

"Why did you agree to come?" he asked, as they were sitting down for the second half. "I mean, the season's practically over."

Clare didn't look at him as she replied.

"Angelo," she muttered.

Clare's younger brother had died in a road accident nearly two years before.

"Did he support County?" Neil asked.

"No," she said, "Sheffield United. I never understood why. But then, I never really understood football, either."

The half began and they watched in silence. United scored and it looked like it was all over. But then something happened. Rather than go out in the humiliating way they'd played all season, County began to counterattack. Within a minute, they'd equalized. The crowd, including Neil, roared. It was the first goal County had scored in weeks. But when Neil looked round at Clare, she wasn't even clapping. She seemed preoccupied – he didn't want to guess with what.

After that, County managed to play a bit. It was 1-1 for half an hour. Then, just when he thought they'd settle for a draw, County got in a lucky header. Now it was United's turn to play for pride, and they pushed forward in the last five minutes, getting a couple of good chances. But they were exposed at the back, and the County centre forward managed to break away, sending a magnificent shot searing into the corner of the net from thirty yards out. The crowd began to sing the Wheelbarrow song, an event reserved for moments of joy or crisis. In this case, it was both. Neil sang along:

"I had a wheelbarrow and the wheel came off..."

He tried to explain the song to Clare. She wasn't interested. The final whistle blew. There was another week and one away game to go, but County's season was effectively over. At least they'd gone out with pride.

One thing about the club having a bad season, it was easier to park near the ground. Five minutes after the whistle, Neil was driving Clare home. Maybe she would invite him in when they got to her house. Or maybe she would plead tiredness and Neil would keep driving, back to Carrington. Neil never put pressure on Clare. In fact, he was getting tired of not putting pressure on Clare. He was hoping she'd ask what he got up to last night, after work. He'd been invited to a party by an attractive nineteen-year-old. Would it make Clare jealous if he told her? Or would she be relieved? For every moment of hope, Neil had a sinking feeling. He felt like he'd called Clare's bluff and any moment now she would fold her cards, leave the game.

They made small talk as Neil drove. Paul Grace had shown up at the pub the night before, Clare said. "He gave me a lift home."

"Didn't try anything on, did he?" Neil asked, the boot suddenly on the other foot.

"You're joking. He's shy, out of uniform. Anyway, Tim thinks he's gay."

"Do you?" Neil asked, surprised.

"I wouldn't know how to tell. He'd keep it really quiet, wouldn't he?"

"Too right."

The police force was full of prejudice. It was bad enough being black, or a woman. Being homosexual was completely beyond the pale. It didn't matter what the Equal Opportunities documents said.

They'd reached Clare's house.

"Coming in?"

"Why not?"

The living-room door was open. Sam, Clare's landlady, sat on the sofa, watching a movie. They said "hello".

"Ruth in?" Clare asked.

"Not back from Ben's yet."

Clare made coffee and they went up to her room.

"Has Sam done anything about renting out the attic?" Neil asked.

"She's put a card up, but she's not optimistic. Wrong time of year."

25

They sat on Clare's single bed. Neil put an arm around Clare, pulling her to him, but she resisted. Sometimes, he wanted her so badly, it actually hurt.

Neil had known Clare for nearly two years. For maybe half of that time, they had gone out with each other. It was an on and off thing, and they had never made love – not once – though there'd been times when they'd come close. When they talked about sex, which wasn't often, Clare said she wanted to wait until she was sure she was *in love*. If they got engaged, Neil thought, it would mean she was in love with him. It would also mean…

Now, when he tried to kiss Clare, his girlfriend pulled away completely.

"This isn't right," she said.

"What does that mean?" Neil said, his face turning red.

She looked at him with her deep, Mediterranean eyes and he knew what was coming.

"I'm sorry," she said.

"*Sorry?* Is this about…?"

Clare nodded slowly, then took a deep breath.

"I care so much for you. I respect you. I can easily see myself being married to you, but…"

Her mouth hung open, too full of pity to finish the sentence. Neil's mouth felt like it was full of stones, but he said it for her anyway.

"You're not in love with me."

"I want to be," Clare told him. "But I'm not."

Neil didn't know what to say. He got up to go.

"I don't want to lose you," Clare said. "There's never been anyone I..."

Neil sighed. Lust had deserted him. He was left with a great emptiness. Had he been fooling himself, all this time?

"We can't stay still," he said. "We either move forward or..."

"It's so hard to explain," Clare said. "I tried to work it out when we split up before. The last thing I want to do is hurt you."

"I know," Neil said. "It's not your fault."

"It's no one's fault."

Clare stood, too. She hugged him. The softness of her body against his was almost too much to bear.

"Don't shut me out," she said.

"I can't," he told her, eyes filling with tears. "You're my best friend."

Clare kept talking, but, after a while, Neil stopped listening. He'd heard her say these things before, the last time they split up. He knew that there was nothing he could say which would make her change her mind. Last time, it had taken him nearly being killed to bring them back together. This time, he knew, there would be no next time. When she ran out of breath, he got up to go.

"Don't see me to the door," he told her, as he turned away. "Goodbye."

3

"You're not going out wearing that!"

Kimberley was wearing cut-off jeans and a skimpy lycra vest, with *Love it. Need it. Want it.* emblazoned across the front. She'd bought the vest in town, with money she got for her thirteenth birthday the week before.

"It's hot," she complained.

"Yes, and your grandad will have a heart attack if he sees your bare navel with that message on top. Put something else on."

"No." Kimberley stomped up to her room and locked the door. The vest had given her the excuse she needed. Ten minutes later, Mum yelled up the stairs.

"Kimberley!"

"Not coming," she yelled back.

"Kimberley, I'll kill you! It's your grandad's birthday."

"If I can't wear what I want, I'm not coming."

The row lasted several minutes, and followed a predictable pattern. It ended with Mum storming out of the house, having issued umpteen threats like, "If your father was here, he'd break the door down." But Dad was with his new family, miles away. Now, Kimberley was free for the evening. Cate, Kimberley's best friend, had told her about a party tonight. It was in the house of a boy from school whose parents were on holiday. Cate was meant to be finding out where the boy lived. But when Kimberley rang Cate, she was already out. Cate's mum said that she was at the church youth group, which was their standard excuse.

"It's OK," Kimberley said. "I'll meet her there."

She went to her bedroom and took off the lycra vest, switching it for something more serious looking, a satin dress which Cate said made her look sexy. In the bathroom, she applied eyeliner and some of her mum's reddest lipstick. Then Kimberley draped a baggy sweater around her shoulders, in case it got cool later. Feeling young, free and pretty, she set out into the estate.

It was still hot and the streets were lively. When the weather was like this, even the Maynard Estate could feel like a film set. Maybe, if Kimberley wandered around, she'd track down the party and find her friend, too. The main action in the estate was at the Three Feathers pub. Made up, Kimberley could pass for fifteen, but they'd throw you out of the Three Feathers unless they were sure you were sixteen. Kimberley walked by the pub anyway. On a hot night like tonight, there were bound to be people outside who she could hang around with.

"Hey, Kim! From school, right?"

Kim recognized the boy. He was in year eleven. Paul something. He was sitting on a bench outside the pub with two of his mates.

"You're looking good, Kim. We've got some cans. Want to join us?"

"All right," Kimberley said. "Why not?"

The boys' smiles were friendly, encouraging. Kimberley sipped lukewarm Kronenborg.

"Do you know anything about a party, later?" she asked.

They didn't.

"But if there's a party, we're up for it," a good-looking Asian boy told her. "D'you know where it is?"

"Only roughly," Kimberley told them.

"We'll find it."

The boys sat on the car park wall, passing the can from hand to hand. When one can was empty, they moved on to the next. Kimberley took small sips. She'd got drunk a couple of times with Cate, didn't like the effect much. The boys talked about music, videos they'd seen. The other white boy was called Darren. The Asian boy's name appeared to be Prak. He kept complimenting Kimberley.

"I can't believe you're only in year eight. You could be a model, anyone ever tell you that?"

"I'm not tall enough," Kimberley told him.

"That's 'cos you're not fully grown yet. Anyone can see you're going to have a great figure. You've got a really good figure now."

Kimberley blushed, excited by the compliments. Cans finished, the four of them decided to look for the party. Kimberley hoped that it wasn't too far away. She needed to be home before Mum. She and Mum usually came home from Grandma and Grandad's at about eleven, just before the pubs closed, when it was still easy to get a taxi.

"Hey, Kimberley," Prak said, walking alongside her, "you're all right." He put an arm around her waist. Prak wasn't from her school, but he must be in year ten or eleven, Kimberley thought. A couple of girls in her year had boyfriends that age. She liked the way that Prak called her by her full name. She liked the fact that he was Asian. His race would really irritate Mum, if she found out about him, although Mum would never admit the reason. Kimberley let his hand stay where it was.

Lorraine hated not having anything to do on

Saturday evenings. If she didn't have a date, she relied on one of the other girls on her floor to be free. They would go round the corner to the Grosvenor on Mansfield Road, where there were usually some other students they knew and often a party to go on to. But, tonight, all the other girls on her corridor were out, or away. Lorraine was forced to go on her own, or stay in, with only her portable TV for company, now that her CD collection had been nicked. She decided to go out on her own.

There was a guy in the corridor, knocking softly on Sophie's door. Lorraine didn't recognize him, which was odd, because she knew most of Sophie's friends. He was older – a third year, she guessed – and well-built, with curly hair. Lorraine couldn't see his face. Then he turned round. He was gorgeous.

"Are you looking for Sophie?" she asked.

He nodded.

"She's gone home for a few days. Ill."

The guy didn't seem surprised, didn't ask what was wrong with Sophie. He didn't even look directly at Lorraine. However, he was so good-looking, she decided to ignore this.

"Are you a friend of hers?" Lorraine asked.

Stupid question. Why else would he be knocking at the door? But he only mumbled, "Sort of."

"I'm Lorraine," she said.

Rudely, he didn't introduce himself, but he fell into step with her as she walked along the corridor, down the stairwell, not speaking.

"I'm surprised the porter let you in," she said, as they crossed the foyer, "since Sophie's signed out home for the weekend. We had a couple of break-ins yesterday. Everyone's very security conscious."

She opened the door, tired of making the running, but kept talking anyway.

"They took all my CDs and a bunch of other stuff."

"Bad luck," the guy muttered, still not looking at her.

"I'm going to the Grosvenor to meet some friends. How about you?"

"This way." He pointed in the opposite direction. "Nice meeting you."

"You too."

He turned back in towards Forest Fields. Oh well, Lorraine thought, you win some, you lose some. She hurried along the road, hoping there would be someone she knew in the pub.

They found the party by the noise, a big old house on the edge of the estate. Kimberley had doubts as soon as they got there. A bloke on the door sent them out to get some booze before he'd let them in. Kimberley wanted to forget it there and then, but Prak persuaded her to stick around. She gave him some money towards the beer. He looked the oldest, so he bought more cans at an offy nearby. When they returned, there was no one on the door, and the place was heaving.

Apart from Paul, Kimberley couldn't see anyone from her school. Maybe this wasn't the party which Cate had been going on about. The place was a tip inside. A couple of windows were boarded up. Kimberley couldn't imagine anyone's parents living there. The four of them opened a can each, because if they put the drinks down, they would be gone in a second.

The music was deafening. Kimberley couldn't make out much of what Prak was saying to her. She leant against the wall and drank from her can. She was trying to drink slowly, but it was stiflingly hot and she was thirsty. The beer began to go to her head. She kept giggling at jokes she could hardly hear. The air was thick with dope. Kimberley knew the smell because Mum smoked it now and then. She and Cate had pinched some once and smoked it. Where was Cate?

Prak's arm remained around Kimberley's waist. Now and then his hand dropped towards her bottom and she moved it back up. She wasn't going to put her free arm around him, not yet, because she didn't want to encourage him too much. She'd discussed this with Cate, although neither of them had had a proper boyfriend yet: give a boy an inch, and he'd take a mile. You had to be really clear about how far they were allowed to go, or they'd go too far.

Now Darren passed Prak a joint. He took his arm from around her waist, had a few drags, then offered the crudely-rolled cigarette to Kimberley. She shook her head.

"Come on," he said. "It'll help you relax."

"I'm relaxed already," Kimberley told him.

"Are you? Then how about a kiss?"

He passed the joint on to Paul, drained his can, then put both arms around Kimberley. She'd been planning on letting him kiss her, maybe if he walked her home. But now she didn't seem to have much choice. His mouth was pressed against hers, and his tongue was intruding into her mouth. It tasted smoky and beery and it wasn't really what she'd expected a first kiss to be like. Kimberley tried to relax and enjoy it.

"I really like you," Prak said, when they broke apart.

"I like you too," Kimberley said.

This wasn't so bad. It was something she could tell Cate about tomorrow. Prak kissed her again. This time, his hand slithered inside her dress, clammy fingers groping bare back. Kimberley broke the kiss.

"Stop!" she said.

"Don't be like that. This is friendly."

"I want you to stop."

"Relax. Take it easy. Enjoy yourself."

His hand stopped moving. Prak kissed her again,

more forcefully. His body pressed hers against the wall. Kimberley could feel him getting worked up, excited. This wasn't what she wanted. She began to struggle.

"Do you want to talk about it yet?" Ruth asked Clare, as they sat in her room. Clare stared into space. She and Ruth had stayed in this Saturday night, even though Ruth was meant to be having a meal with Ben. Ruth's boyfriend and Clare's ex-boyfriend had gone out drinking together, a last minute arrangement which Ruth resented, but understood.

"How did he take it?" Ruth asked.

"He cried," Clare said, quietly.

"And…?"

"And I talked a bit more, until I ran out of things to say. Then he got up and left."

"How did you leave things?"

Clare shrugged. "Friends, whatever that means."

"You know what that means."

"Do I?" Clare asked. "Seems to me that all the men I've known since school have either been boyfriends or friends of boyfriends, not my friends in their own right. I've finished with Neil and who have I got, outside work? You. Sam, maybe. Then there's all the people I used to know but hardly see since I joined the force."

"You're not allowed to feel sorry for yourself,"

Ruth told her. "After all, you chucked him. And you always have plenty of men after you."

"Sorry," Clare said. "You're right. Neil gets to mope about the end of the relationship. I don't."

She stood up. "Let's go for a drink."

"Fine," Ruth said. "Where shall we go? The Grosvenor? That's always lively on a Saturday night."

"No," Clare told her. "I want somewhere quiet. Anyway, Neil and Ben might be at the Grosvenor. I don't want to bump into them."

"Fair enough," Ruth said. "Let's join Sam in the Carlton."

But, when they got to the pub, they didn't join Sam, because she was talking to Steve, her ex-lover and ex-lodger, who still lived somewhere in the area. Steve gave the two young women a surly look, reminding them that they were police officers, and not to be trusted. Ruth got the feeling that a majority of people in the bar felt the same way. Why was it that they only ever felt really comfortable around other cops?

After two drinks, Ruth and Clare retreated home to watch the evening movie. It was a thriller. The villains were really bad, and the cops really stupid, but a brave, resourceful civilian saved the day, rescued the girl, then walked off with her and a million dollars which everyone else seemed to have forgotten about.

"Doesn't it make you feel really good about yourself and the job that you do?" Clare asked, sarcastically.

"Don't take everything so seriously," Ruth complained. "It's only a movie. Mind if we watch Match of the Day?"

"Not more football," Clare protested. But she let Ruth put it on, started yawning, and, pretty soon, went to bed. Ruth stayed up, watching the dregs of the season, worrying about Clare and wondering whether Ben would show up.

"Leave her alone."

Someone was grabbing Prak and pulling him off her.

"Mind your own..."

Prak turned round and realized that the guy was older, bigger than him.

"She's not interested in you, you..."

The guy let loose a stream of swear words and racist jibes, all of which Kimberley knew, but which she had never heard in such a colourful combination before. Then he punched Prak in the gut. The last Kimberley saw of Prak that night, he was leaning over an already filthy sink, vomiting.

"You all right?"

Kimberley nodded. Her eyes were wet with tears. She could barely see her rescuer.

"I want to go home," she said.

"Yeah, I'll take you. There's no phone in this dump, but me mate's got a mobile. I'll call a taxi. Want to sit down for a bit? We can't have you going home in a state like this, can we? Want to wash your face?"

Kimberley nodded gratefully. The guy took her hand and led Kimberley upstairs, to the bathroom.

"I'll watch the door," said the bloke, in a gentle voice. "No towel, I'm afraid. Here."

He pulled off his T-shirt as she splashed water on to her face.

"You can use this. I was feeling too hot anyway."

Gratefully, Kimberley dried herself.

"What's your name?"

"Kimberley."

"Mind if I call you Kim? Like Kim Basinger. It's a nice name."

"No. I don't mind."

"What's a nice girl like you doing in a dump like this, Kim?"

It was such an old line that Kimberley couldn't help smiling. Her protector smiled back. She held out his T-shirt.

"Thanks."

"You're welcome," he said, his voice suddenly deeper.

Instead of taking the T-shirt, he took Kimberley's hand, gently pulling her towards him. Her body trembling, Kimberley gave him a weak smile.

*   *   *

"Another?"

Ben had been matching Neil pint for pint, but his were shandies, so he was sober, and Neil wasn't. Ben was fed up with being cast as an expert on Clare Coppola, simply because he happened to work with the woman. He could have told Neil months ago that he wouldn't hang on to her. Clare was too young, too sexy and too impatient to settle for Neil, or, indeed, anyone, yet. Ben got these insights not from working with Clare, but from his girlfriend, Ruth. The picture Ruth painted was one of chronic indecision, laced with ambition. Clare didn't know what she wanted, but she wanted it fast.

When Ben got back to the table, a top-heavy blonde was having a few words with Neil. She smiled at Ben as she walked away.

"Not wasting any time," Ben teased his friend.

"Burglary victim, yesterday," Neil said. "Lorraine something. She wanted to know if we'd found anything."

"Not bad," Ben said.

"Not my type. Though there was this girl in the same hall…" Neil smiled ruefully. "If I'd known last night that I was single…" Then his face fell and he took a huge gulp of his pint. When he went to the loo, his feet were less steady than his voice had been.

"Come on," Ben said. "Time to go home."

Neil nodded. "Coming back for coffee?"

"Sure."

Neil got up and left without finishing his pint. Ben half carried him home, which, luckily, wasn't far away. He didn't want coffee, but would make sure that Neil got safely to bed. That was what friends were for. Then, if it wasn't too late, he would go round to Ruth's, as they'd agreed earlier. Like him, she was a night owl, and needed less sleep than most. For the two of them, the night was still young.

The taxi deposited Kimberley outside her house at twenty past eleven. She ran inside. Luckily, Mum wasn't back yet. Upstairs, Kimberley took off her sweater and threw her torn dress into the laundry basket. Then she went and had a shower. When Mum returned, fifteen minutes later, Kimberley was tucked up in bed with the light off, and the door locked. Mum called out a couple of times, then left it. The door only locked from the inside. Her daughter, she would think, must be home, and was probably still sulking.

Kimberley lay under the duvet in her warm room on the warmest night of the year so far. She couldn't stop shivering.

4

Clare hated giving talks, always had. Today she was revisiting her old school to talk to a year-eight tutor group about personal safety. This used to be the job of a Community Liaison PC. However, the last one had left the force to train to be a teacher and they hadn't replaced her. So, now, everyone had to pitch in. Clare was on a two till ten today, and wouldn't get overtime for turning up this morning, only Brownie points with the boss. She hoped that Paul Grace appreciated her.

Clare hated giving talks, always had. Today she was revisiting her old school to talk to a year-eight tutor group about personal safety. This used to be the job of a Community Liaison PC. However, the last one had left the force to train to be a teacher and they hadn't replaced her. So, now, everyone had to pitch in. Clare was on a two till ten today, and wouldn't get overtime for turning up this morning, only Brownie points with the boss. She hoped that Paul Grace appreciated her.

The teacher was new. Clare didn't know her. But she knew the classroom. It brought back boring, repetitive maths lessons, three times a week for five long years.

"This is Constable Coppola. She was a pupil at

Greencoat, not many years ago. Today, she's going to talk to you about personal safety."

Clare began haltingly. To get their attention, she threw out a few statistics about violence in the city. The people who got attacked in the streets weren't old ladies, getting mugged. They were young men, being attacked by other young men. Often, alcohol was involved. Sometimes, weapons. The best defence wasn't attack, no matter what your macho friends said. It was running away.

She moved on to women, and the dangers of walking home alone at night. Stick to well-lit streets, Clare told the thirteen-year-olds. Don't take short cuts, and walk on the side of the road where you face oncoming traffic. Have your keys in your hand – they're a good weapon. Best of all, don't walk home alone.

"You don't always have a choice," one girl pointed out.

"I know," Clare said, "and everybody ought to have the right to walk the streets unmolested. But Nottingham is a big city, with all the advantages and disadvantages which go with that, one of them being a high crime rate. So, use your common sense – when you need to be out alone, it's worth carrying a personal safety alarm. But don't worry needlessly. Despite what you might hear, it's unusual for women to be attacked by strangers. Seventy per cent of rapists aren't strangers in the street, they're people who the victim already knows."

"So how do you tell which ones to avoid?" a short-haired girl asked.

"Good question," Clare said. "But I'm afraid I don't have the answer to it."

What should she tell them? Not to trust any man, until you knew him really well? It was probably the truth, but it was too depressing to unleash on kids barely out of childhood. Especially as childhood seemed to end earlier and earlier these days.

"Any more questions?" Clare looked around. She had their attention. That was good. All except for one girl who sat by the window, her pale face masked by long, blonde hair. She seemed to be staring at the desk.

"What about safety *from* the police?" a loud-mouthed boy asked. "What if you get pulled over on the street and they want to search you for drugs? That happened to a mate of mine. They knocked him about."

"If the officers involved used any form of violence," Clare said, carefully, "then I hope your mate complained."

A flood of questions followed. The tutor period was soon over. Clare finished with a little homily.

"Remember," she said, "no matter what you've heard, the police are here to help you. I mean that. If you have a crime-related problem, pick up the phone and dial three nines. Better still, stop an officer on the beat. Or come to the station. You all know where it is. We're here to help."

"That was excellent," the teacher said, afterwards. "I'll tell the other tutors how good it was. I'm sure they'll all want you to come in."

"Thank you," Clare said, cursing inwardly.

She watched as the last of the class trailed out. The girl with the long blonde hair was accompanied by the girl with the short, dark crop who'd asked the first question. She was trying to talk to the blonde girl, failing.

"Are you sure you're all right?" Clare heard the dark girl saying. Then the teacher started talking again and Clare didn't hear the girl's reply.

At break, Cate finally got Kimberley on her own.

"You missed a great party," Cate told Kimberley in the year eight social area. "What happened to you? I rang yesterday, but your mum said you were ill in bed."

"I couldn't find you," Kimberley muttered. "I didn't know where it was."

"Mum insisted on dropping me off at Youth Group," Cate explained, her voice a little guilty. "Meg knew the address. She went round for you, but there was no one in. We thought you couldn't get out of going to your grandparents."

Kimberley continued to let her hair hang forward, so that Cate couldn't see the expression on her face.

"So what *did* you do?" Cate asked.

"I looked for the party," Kimberley mumbled. "I found a party."

"On your own?"

Guilt changed to concern. Kimberley shook her head.

"Some lads from school."

"Which lads?"

Instead of answering, Kimberley looked away, out of the window, over the fields, towards where it had happened.

Neil didn't like working an eight to four shift. It meant that his evenings were long and empty. Most of the other officers in Neil's unit had families. Neil had only a mother in Wollaton. The day before he'd had the awkward experience of explaining to his mum that she wouldn't be seeing Clare any more. The woman Mum hoped would be her daughter-in-law was now merely Neil's ex-girlfriend. For some reason, having to tell his mum this upset Neil more than Clare had upset him the day before.

Now that it was over, Neil wanted to throw himself into his work, to get his teeth into a good case, like the arsons a few weeks ago. But all he had on the go were some petty thefts from students' rooms. There was never going to be any overtime in that. He was stuck in the office all day, catching up on paperwork from last week. At four, he would finish,

46

and the long, Clare-less evening would stretch ahead of him.

"Call for you, Neil."

He picked up the phone and there was a Brummie accent on the other end.

"Are you the officer dealing with the thefts at Wordsworth Hall?"

"Yes. What can I do for you?"

"I think my room was broken into."

"Think?" Neil said, impatiently. "Aren't you sure?"

"The only thing missing is my credit card. I never use it. I keep it in the pages of ... a book."

"You've probably lost it," Neil said. "Things fall out of books. Maybe –"

"It's just that I heard about the burglaries..."

"Are you sure there's nothing else missing? Was anything disturbed in any way?"

Both no.

"All right then. Have another good look. If there's nothing else missing, call the credit card company, tell them you've lost the card. They'll check if there's been any abnormal activity on your card before they issue a new one. If there has, ring me again. OK?"

"OK. Thank you."

Neil went back to typing up his report. Much as he hated paperwork, the last thing he wanted to do was trek over to Forest Fields to deal with a lost credit card. What came next? Missing cats?

The thief sat in the magistrates' court, facing the bench. When the time came, he pleaded guilty to two charges of theft, with two other charges taken into consideration. Because he was pleading guilty, there were no witnesses in court, only prosecuting counsel, the thief's solicitor and a probation officer. The thief was glad to see that the press bench was empty. Most of his friends had no idea about his recent trouble, and he intended to keep it that way.

The prosecution case was swift and to the point.

"This is a young man with every advantage," the barrister concluded, "who has nevertheless committed a series of callous, contemptible crimes on his neighbours, all of them motivated by greed. Given the number of these offences, a prison sentence must be a foregone conclusion."

The thief was shaken. His solicitor had told him that there was no possibility of prison. But suppose he'd got a tough bunch of magistrates? Suppose they decided to make an example of him?

The thief came from a good family background, the defence solicitor told the court, and was of previous good character. Unemployed, and at a low ebb, he had yielded to temptation, not realizing the seriousness of his crimes. He treated his burglaries as a schoolboy lark and, when he realized the effects of his misdeeds, made efforts to return some of the goods. A custodial sentence was wholly inappropriate. The thief now spent much of his time working voluntarily for the homeless. Being caught had taught him a lesson. Having a criminal record was punishment enough in itself.

The magistrates retired briefly to consider their verdict. The solicitor told the thief not to worry. The thief wasn't worried. It was true, being caught had taught him a lesson: *don't get caught again*. And it had confirmed him in his course of career. He would never get a decent job with two convictions for theft.

But the thief wasn't worried about that now. He was worried about the girl called Sophie, who he'd stumbled into three days before. He knew what had happened to Sophie on Friday afternoon, and he had seen the person who did it. He had comforted Sophie afterwards, until she asked him to go.

What the thief didn't know was whether Sophie had reported the rape. And if she did report it, had she told the police about his presence in the hall? Sophie didn't know why the thief was in Wordsworth Hall that day. However, if she'd told the police, they were bound to have worked it out by now. They'd want him, both as a witness, and as a burglary suspect.

The thief couldn't go forward with a witness statement, but he wanted to help. He didn't know what to do about it: an anonymous phone call, perhaps, giving a description of the attacker? A letter to CID?

The magistrates came back out. There were two middle-aged women and an old man. The man, of course, did the talking. He spoke like an army officer, or the head of a very old, established public school.

"We have listened carefully to the prosecution case and the points made by the defence in deciding your sentence. We hope that your solicitor is right, and you have learnt your lesson. In view of your previous good character, we have decided that you will be sentenced to six months' imprisonment for each offence, suspended for two years. Therefore, if you are returned to this court and found guilty of any offence, you face a year's imprisonment, on top of whatever other sentence you receive. Do you understand?"

"Yes, your honour."

"You will also pay a hundred and twenty pounds costs."

When it was over the thief shook hands with his solicitor and went round the corner to the Treasury, where he paid his costs in cash. He'd been expecting to pay more, so had plenty of money left over from the credit card advance he'd got that morning.

It was a bright sunny day, so the thief decided to walk home. The suspended sentence changed things, he decided as he walked. If he got caught again, he could well go down. He couldn't give up, but he must be even more careful. So he would stay well away from Wordsworth Hall. The rapist wasn't his business. There would be no anonymous reports to the police. On his way up the hill, the thief passed a drain. He wiped the stolen credit card so that there'd be no prints, then dropped the thing into darkness. He'd already had over four hundred quid's worth of stuff from it, and, now that he had a suspended sentence, he wasn't going to take any unnecessary risks.

5

"Hey, Kimberley!" a voice called from the lunch queue.

Reluctantly, she turned round. It was Paul from Saturday night.

"Have a good time, did you?"

Walking by Kimberley, Cate gave her a funny look.

"You didn't get off with him, did you?"

Kimberley shook her head. Paul kept yelling.

"My mate Prak really liked you, you know?"

"Come on!" Kimberley said, tugging Cate's school shirt.

Since Kimberley was ignoring him, Paul began to talk loudly to the person next to him in the queue.

"You wouldn't think it to look at her, but she's a real goer, Kimberley is. My mate Prak thought he was in there, but Kimberley prefers older blokes. Don't you, Kimberley?"

He called out these last three words in a loud, taunting voice.

"Come on," Kimberley said.

"What about lunch?" Cate said.

"Sod lunch."

As they turned the corner, Paul's closing word shot across the quadrangle.

"Slut!"

"Who's Prak?" Cate asked, when they were clear of the crowds.

"A boy I met on Saturday. I went to the party with him and Paul and some other bloke."

"You got off with him?"

"I guess."

Cate gave Kimberley a searching look.

"What did you do?"

Kimberley folded her arms and wrapped them tightly around herself, until she felt like she was wearing a strait-jacket.

"God," Cate said, her face registering a mixture of concern and curiosity, "you didn't *do it* with him, did you?"

Kimberley shook her head. "I did like we said. But he'd been drinking. He had his hands all over me. I wasn't scared, but he was a bit rough. I told him to stop. Then this other guy came along…"

"The older one?"

"And he … and he…" Kimberley burst into tears.

"What happened?" Cate asked, putting an arm around her. "What happened?"

The second phone call came an hour later, just as Neil was about to take a lunch break.

"I called earlier," the Brummie accent said. "My name's Mark Brewer. I live in Wordsworth Hall. You told me to contact the credit card company."

"Oh, yes. Any news?"

"The card was used at least twice over the weekend – probably a lot more, they said. And it was used again this morning. Whoever stole it got a cash advance of two hundred and fifty quid."

"I'm on my way round," Neil told him.

Before driving over to Wordsworth Hall, Neil had a word with Chris Dylan.

"It's probably your burglar using the card," Dylan said. "He didn't have time to sell it to a middleman. Get on to it as quickly as possible. If you can get a decent description and he's stupid enough to use the card again, we might have a chance of nabbing him."

"There is another possibility," Neil said.

"What?"

"That this Mark Brewer heard about the burglaries and decided to try it on. He went on a spending spree with his own card, then reported it stolen when he'd reached the credit limit."

Dylan agreed. "Mastercard would only charge him twenty-five quid for reporting the theft late, so he'd still be several hundred pounds to the good. It's possible. Take one of the instant cameras with you and get a snap of Brewer. Then you'll have something to show the shops when you do the rounds later on."

Neil's suspicions of Mark Brewer began to dematerialize as soon as he saw the youth's room. It was spartan. The things which had been bought on his card – beer, spirits, CDs – were not things which seemed to fit in with Mark's lifestyle.

"Where were you over the weekend?" Neil asked.

"I went to London. There was this big Methodist rally in Hyde Park. You know, there were thousands and thousands of people there, but did it get into the papers? Not a word. If we'd been at a rave, or protesting against the Criminal Justice Act…"

"Most people would have taken their credit card with them."

"I rarely use it," Mark explained. "It's only for emergencies and special occasions. There was a coach to and from the rally. I'd taken packed food."

"All right," Neil said. "When did you last see the card?"

"Last week. It was only the second time I'd used it. I bought some rugby tickets over the phone."

"And then you put the card back in the Bible?"

"Yes."

"Did anyone else know where you kept the card?"

"No."

Neil examined the lock on the door. Like Melanie Byatt's it could easily have been broken into with a screwdriver or plastic card. There was little point in fingerprinting three days after the event.

"Do you mind if I take your photograph?" he asked the student.

"Why?"

"I need to show it to shopkeepers at places where the card was used, in order to eliminate you from our inquiries."

"You don't think that I..."

"No. It's standard procedure."

Neil took the photograph then got away as quickly as he could. He needed to get around the shops, see if he could come up with a description. There was no chance of overtime on a job like this, but his shift still had three hours to run. He wanted a description before the day was out.

He didn't have to wait that long. In the foyer, he bumped into Lorraine Parker.

"I've been meaning to call you," she said. "I nearly said something on Saturday night, but you seemed a bit—"

"Thought of something else that's missing?" Neil interrupted her.

"No, but I think I might have seen who did it."

"Who?"

"There was this guy, knocking on my friend Sophie's door on Saturday night. It was a really gentle knock, like he didn't want to be heard. I came by, and told him that Sophie had gone home for the weekend. Then I walked downstairs with him. I tried to get him talking and he was a bit … not mysterious exactly, but he wouldn't say much. It was only yesterday that I was thinking – who let him into the building? The porter would know that Sophie was out. And if he was a friend of hers, why hadn't she mentioned him to me? He was kind of memorable looking."

"You think he might have been the thief?"

"Yes."

Neil scratched his chin. "I have to say that it's unlikely he would come back so quickly, but you never know. Could you describe this man for me?"

"I'll do my best. He had this leather jacket, for a start…"

An hour later, Neil was in WH Smith's in the Victoria Centre. He had already been to the bank where the thief had got a credit card cash advance that morning. No one remembered him. The woman in the music section said that, yes, she had been working on Saturday. Neil showed her his warrant card.

"A man came in here at about three in the afternoon, spent nearly fifty pounds on a green mastercard in the name of Mark Brewer. Would you happen to remember him?"

"We have so many customers. Saturday's our busiest time."

Neil showed her the photo of Mark Brewer. "Is this man familiar?"

"No."

Then Neil repeated the description which Lorraine had given him. When he got to the man's jacket, the woman interrupted.

"Yes, I remember him now. He wasn't one of our usual kind of customers. And the sort of thing he was buying, he could have bought a lot more cheaply elsewhere. He looked like the sort of person who'd know that."

He would have shopped here because staff in the specialist record shops would recognize him, Neil guessed. They might know that his name wasn't Mark Brewer.

"Can you describe him in your own words?"

"He was about twenty-two, I'd say. He was wearing one of those leather jackets with the sheepskin on the outside – what do you call them? A flying jacket. He was quite well built. He had brown, curly hair, below the ears, strong jaw, good-looking, really – average height, maybe a bit taller."

Neil smiled.

"Gotcha!" he said.

* * *

"You've got two visitors," Inspector Grace told Clare, as she was catching up on her paperwork. "Two young ladies. Asked for you personally."

"Oh. Right."

Clare went down to the foyer. Although they weren't in school uniform, she immediately recognized the two girls from the morning, one with long blonde hair, the other with short dark hair. Clare asked their names and was told them.

"You said to come if we had a problem," Cate began.

"Of course. Do you want to talk somewhere private? There's an interview room over here."

The girls followed Clare into the small, pale green space.

"Do your parents know you're here?" Clare asked, gently.

Both girls shook their head. Clare would have to be careful. There were strict guidelines about what you could do when parents weren't present. But she had to find out what the problem was first. For all she knew, the parents could be behind it.

"Tell me why you've come," Clare said.

Cate looked at Kimberley. The younger-looking girl's mouth opened and closed, but she remained silent.

"Take your time," Clare said.

A single tear streaked down Kimberley's face.

"It's Kimberley," Cate announced, her voice wobbling with emotion. "She's been raped."

6

The manager of the off-licence confirmed the description Neil already had. The thief had bought forty pounds worth of beer, vodka and bourbon there. Back at the CID office, Chris Dylan arranged for the card details and description to be given to every major supermarket and off-licence within two miles of the city centre.

"He's local," Neil said, "we know that. So he'll avoid going to places where he usually goes, where they'll know he's not Mark Brewer."

"I hate to put a damper on this," Chris told him, "but if our lad's halfway professional, he'll have dumped that card by now."

Neil guessed that his boss was right, but it had to be worth taking a chance.

"Maybe our burglar's stupid," he suggested. "Most are. We might get lucky."

"Maybe," Dylan retorted. "But I'd look for another angle. This guy seems to know his way around a hall of residence which has fairly good security. He's aged between twenty and twenty-five. Does that suggest anything to you?"

"You think he could be an ex-student?"

"They have their own keys to get in, right? Suppose this guy held on to his, or had it copied? Later, he starts using it."

"So if I get a list of former students who've lived in the hall... It's only been open two or three years, so it shouldn't be a long list," Neil said, thinking aloud. "Give all the names a PNC check..."

"Then go and see the ones who've got a criminal record. But this guy's so brazen, I doubt he's ever been caught. So you'll need to do another check with university admin., see how many male former students still live in Nottingham, check their photographs to see if they match the description you've got..."

"It might take a while."

Dylan gave him a sour grin. "That's what they call detective work."

Neil checked his watch. It was nearly time to knock off. "I'll start first thing in the morning, if that's all right with you."

Dylan considered for a few seconds, then nodded.

"I'll give you a couple more days to run with it."

The phone rang.

"DS Dylan."

Neil watched as the sergeant's face turned grave. He could only hear one side of the conversation.

"There's only me and my oppo here now. When? Why's she being interviewed at home? How old? All right. We're on it."

He put down the phone.

"Forget everything I just said," he told Neil. "I need you to do some overtime with me. New case."

"Now?"

Dylan nodded and pulled on his coat.

"The boss has gone home. I'll get him to approve the overtime tomorrow."

Neil followed the detective sergeant to his car.

"What's the case?"

"Rape. A thirteen-year-old girl."

Neil blasphemed.

"It happened on Saturday night," Dylan continued. "She's only just reported it."

"Ouch."

"I washed the dress," Kimberley's mother was telling Jan Hunt. "I didn't notice the rip. It's waiting to be ironed."

She sat on the sofa, scratching her thighs with her hands. Clare found this action unsettling.

"What if she's pregnant? What if he's given her some disease?"

"Kimberley isn't sure whether the man who did this wore a condom," Jan told Karen Pierce. "It's unlikely he did. So a doctor ought to give her emergency contraception. It's effective up to seventy-two hours after intercourse."

"What if he's given her AIDS?"

"It's unlikely," Jan said. "Really."

Kimberley's mother dug her nails deeper into her thighs, leaving thin red weals.

"Please," Clare said, reaching over. "Don't do that, Karen. You're hurting yourself."

"He hurt my baby. You'll catch him, won't you?"

"I hope so," Clare said. "I hope so."

"She's only a child."

Since Kimberley was under sixteen, she had to be questioned with an appropriate adult present. This was why Jan and Clare had brought her home. Clare would take Kimberley's statement. She'd done the rape awareness course which was part of the two-year training these days. Jan hadn't.

As soon as they'd got her home, Kimberley had burst into tears. Clare and Jan had had to explain to Karen Pierce why they were there. Mother and daughter had been alone for several minutes. Now Kimberley was in the bathroom, with her friend, Cate, washing her face.

"She'll be down in a minute," Cate said,

returning downstairs.

"Why don't I take you home, love?" Jan suggested. "I've got a few questions to ask you, too."

Before she left, Jan asked Karen Pierce whether she wanted the police to contact Kimberley's father and grandparents.

"Her father's working away. We're divorced. Her grandfather – my dad – he's in the job."

"Locally?"

"His name's Roy Tate."

"I know him," Clare said. "He's Ruth's partner."

"Will he … will he already know?"

"We don't give out victims' names in cases like these," Jan said, "not even to other police officers."

"Would you like us to get him?" Clare suggested. "I'm sure that he'd want to be here with you."

"No," Karen said, sobbing. "I can't tell him yet. He'll go mad. Dad's always saying I give Kimberley too much freedom. He'll say it's my fault. She should have been with him and Mum that evening. It was his birthday."

"It's hard to tell young girls what to do these days," Jan commented, tactfully, before leaving with Cate.

While they waited for Kimberley, Clare asked some more questions. Karen Pierce, however, had little to tell her. She and her daughter had had a row on Saturday night, but Kimberley was home when

Karen got in, at about eleven-thirty. The girl stayed in her room most of Sunday, claiming to have a stomach-ache. Karen thought she was sulking about something. It sounded like a typical relationship between a single mother and an adolescent girl.

When Kimberley came downstairs, she looked like an ill child, not a young woman. The thought of what had happened to her made Clare feel sick. Even so, she had to sound calm and reassuring, concerned, but in control. Kimberley sat on the sofa next to her mother.

"I'm going to take your statement," Clare said. "And then, if you're up to it, I'm going to get a police surgeon to look at you."

Two days on, there was little chance of physical evidence which was worth anything, but they had to try. Some rape victims, Clare knew, hated being examined by a doctor. Kimberley looked too numb to care.

Several hours later, Clare and Jan took Kimberley and her mother to the Victim Examination Suite at Oxclose Lane. Their job was done, for now, but Clare had to go back to CID and liaise with the officers who'd been assigned to the case. Jan drove her.

"Roy's bound to find out sooner or later," Clare said, in a quiet voice.

"I don't want to be the one to tell him," Jan replied.

"But what about Ruth?" Clare protested. "If I tell her, but she can't tell Roy, it'll make things really awkward between them."

"So don't tell her."

Clare sighed. "I guess I'd better not."

In CID, Neil Foster and Chris Dylan were about to start an interview. Jan stayed while Clare gave Chris a summary of Kimberley's statement. Chris asked a few questions, then told Clare to make sure she kept in touch with the girl and her mother. All the time they were there, Neil barely said a word to Jan or Clare.

"What did we do?" Jan asked, as they both went off duty for the evening. Clare felt choked up inside. Compared to the rape of a young girl, her break up with Neil seemed insignificant. She had been on the force for over six months now, but this was the first such crime she'd handled.

"There's something I haven't got round to telling you," Clare admitted.

Neil and Chris were into their fourth hour of overtime. They'd already interviewed Paul Fox, the boy from Kimberley's school who went to the party with her. The only useful information they'd got from him was the address of Prak, the youth who Kimberley spent some time kissing that Saturday night. Prakesh wouldn't talk at home – he didn't want his parents hearing what he'd been up to with a white girl – so they had him in an interview room at the station.

"All right, Prakesh," Chris Dylan was saying. "Let's go over this one more time. You were with Kimberley and some bloke grabs you, lands you on the floor."

"That's right."

"No reason?"

"I dunno. He must have fancied her. What's this about?"

"Never mind that. I want a full description of the guy who hit you."

Prakesh pulled a face. "I don't remember. I'd been drinking, right? He was bigger than me, white, dark hair. Look, I don't want to press charges, so what's the point?"

"How much bigger than you?"

Prakesh was only five-seven.

"Not much taller, but heavier, you know what I mean? He looked heavy. That's all I remember."

"We want you to make a list of all the people you remember who were at the party."

"You're kidding! I only stayed half an hour. The only people whose names I know are the ones I went with."

"We'd still like you to try, please."

While Prakesh took his time with a pen and paper, Chris and Neil reviewed what they'd got. Paul Fox claimed not to have seen the bloke who attacked

Prakesh. Maybe this was true, or maybe he was scared. They hadn't found the other boy, Darren, yet. It was possible that he'd seen something. They'd also learnt from Kimberley's statement that the rapist had put her into a taxi afterwards. He'd paid the cab in advance. Kimberley couldn't remember which taxi firm he'd used, but finding the driver shouldn't be too difficult.

Then there were the other people at the party. The house had been squatted at various times, but its occupants had moved on rather than tackle the colossal mess the party left behind. Neighbours reported that the noise lasted until dawn, although none had reported it to the police or the Environmental Health.

It was that kind of area. If Kimberley had reported the attack as soon as she got home, things would have been a lot easier. As it was, the squat's occupants, and the other party goers, could be scattered across the city.

Neil took the list of descriptions from Prakesh. It was less than useless. Neil knew from Kimberley's statement that the boy had been smoking cannabis, which wouldn't help his memory. But CID weren't interested in drugs. They were interested in whether the sixteen-year-old boy was holding anything back.

"You and your friends took Kimberley to this party, Prakesh. Wasn't it your responsibility to look after her? Why did you leave without her?"

"She'd gone off with someone else, hadn't she?"

"How did you know that?"

"Because..." The boy hesitated.

"Did someone tell you?"

"I don't remember."

"Try to remember."

"I don't..."

"How did you know she was with someone else?"

"I guessed that she was with the guy who hit me, all right?"

"Why?"

"Why else would he hit me? He wanted her, right. Look, what's all this about? I knew she was under age. I didn't do anything. Kimberley'll back me up on that. Won't she? What's all this about?"

"Rough shift?"

Ruth was on a rest day because she was about to start nights. Clare had come in at twenty past ten, looking shattered.

"Yeah," Clare said. "It's been a long day. I had to do that school talk at nine, then go back on at two."

"I don't know how you do that, going back to your old school."

"It's on my beat."

"I don't know how you do that, either."

Clare shrugged. "You're the one who lives in the area you patrol."

"Point taken."

Ruth accepted that living in Forest Fields was a little weird. Other officers on her beat sometimes teased her about it. But she'd wanted to share a house with Clare, and this was the first one that came up.

"Coming for a drink?" Ruth suggested. "Our last chance to get out together for a week."

"Go on then," Clare said. "Give me a minute to change."

In the Carlton, their landlady, Sam, was already sitting in a corner with Steve. Clare and Ruth didn't join them.

"That makes twice this week," Clare complained, as she brought the drinks over. "Are they getting back together or something?"

"He was in court today," Ruth explained, "for the burglaries in our street. Sam mentioned it earlier. She's meeting him to find out how it went."

"Obviously, he didn't get prison."

"Maybe we should go over, ask…"

"Aren't you forgetting something?" Clare said.

Ruth knew what she was getting at. "That you arrested him? No, I've not forgotten. But he's been to court. He's taken his punishment, whatever it was. Why shouldn't we treat him like we'd treat anybody else?"

"Because he's a stupid thief."

Ruth shook her head. "All that time you spend with Jan Hunt is making you as cynical as her."

"It's not Jan," Clare said. "It's the job."

Clare seemed to be in a black mood, so Ruth decided not to press the point. Splitting up with Neil must be hurting her more than she was letting on. Ruth watched as Steve picked up his tatty flying jacket from the floor and walked out of the pub without looking in her direction. Once he was through the door, Sam came over to join them.

"What did he get?" Ruth asked.

"Two six-month sentences, suspended, and costs."

"He got off lightly," Clare said.

"It was a first offence," Sam pointed out.

"How's he taken it?" Ruth enquired.

"I don't know," Sam said. "He's talking about moving, making a new start somewhere else. But he doesn't have a clue about what kind of job to do."

"There's always a life of crime," Clare said, with no humour in her voice. Ruth glared at her friend. Sam knew that Steve was a loser. There was no need to rub it in.

"Any joy in letting out his room?" Ruth asked.

"Nothing," Sam said. "I'm thinking of putting an ad in the paper."

"For a woman?"

"I don't know," Sam said. "Does it have to be a woman?"

"It's your house," Ruth told her. "It's up to you."

"I've always made it a principle to consult the

other tenants before taking in a new one. What do you think, Clare?"

Clare had been looking away, distracted. "Pardon?"

"You think we should be looking for another woman to fill the attic room?"

"Man, woman, it's all the same to me."

"Actually," Ruth said. "I've been meaning to ask. That attic room, it's a lot bigger than mine. Would it be all right if I moved into it?"

"But you've only just got your room sorted out," Clare protested.

"I know," Ruth said. "But that one's more private, too … and quieter. Like, this week, when I'm on night shift, it'd be easier to sleep…" And she would have more privacy with Ben too, when he came round.

"It's fine by me," Sam said.

"And me," Clare said.

"That's settled, then."

"I'll help you move in the morning, if you like," Clare offered.

"Thanks," Ruth told them both.

Back home, Ruth tried to persuade Clare to stay up late with her and watch a movie. The later Ruth stayed up, the easier it would be to adapt to the night shift the next day. But Clare said she was too tired, and went to bed. Ruth rang up Ben, and talked to him for twenty minutes, whispering in the hall.

"Clare seemed a bit down today," she said to her boyfriend.

"Did she?" Ben asked, then changed the subject quickly.

Ruth wondered if there was something Clare wasn't telling her.

7

"Are you sure this is a good idea," Cate asked Kimberley as they walked in together, "coming straight back to school?"

"The police said it was OK," Kimberley told her. "What else am I supposed to do – stay home on my own?"

But the day was awful. No one was meant to know, but, somehow, word had spread about what had happened. Kids kept pointing at Kimberley. She heard whispers. The only person who spoke to her directly was Mrs Marshall, her form teacher. All she said was, "Are you sure that you want to be in school today?" Then, when Kimberley said she was sure, "If you ever need to talk about it…"

But it was clear that Mrs Marshall didn't really

want to talk about it, and neither did Kimberley. At least, not with her.

Kimberley wasn't used to getting attention. Cate sometimes mouthed off in class. Although Kimberley knew just as many answers, she preferred to watch her friend take the limelight. Occasionally, Cate made a fool of herself, but didn't seem to mind. Kimberley would have hated it. Today, it felt like she had humiliated herself in front of the entire school. Teachers she didn't know stared as she walked down the corridors: *is she the one?* Cate stuck to Kimberley like glue.

"If only I'd come round for you," she kept saying, even though both of them knew that it wasn't remotely her fault.

Cate couldn't ward off all the busybodies, the drama queens who kept coming up, pretending to offer sympathy, actually wanting details. One girl who Kimberley barely knew burst into tears. "It's not fair," she kept saying. "It's not fair." Cate had to practically push her away. She took to swearing at people who were bugging Kimberley.

"She just wants to be left alone. You weren't interested in her yesterday, so leave her alone today."

But even the girls who were supposed to be her friends became weird.

"What was it like," Kelly asked, "losing your virginity?" As though what had happened to her had something to do with sex. *It wasn't sex!* Kimberley wanted to scream. *It was violence!* But there was no point in trying to explain. When they didn't understand, she would feel even lonelier.

The boys were a hundred times worse than the girls. The ones in her class took ages to work out what was going on. Most of them ignored Kimberley, which was fine. Only Colin Cook, who had less brains than a butterfly, came up to her and said, "It isn't true, is it?" as though the whole thing was one great big joke. When he saw the look she gave him, his face went red and he ran off.

But the older boys looked at her like she was a whore. She heard the words they were using: slag, scrubber, slut. They didn't try to keep their voices down. Who had told on her? The only people she had talked to were Cate and Mrs Marshall. Was it the teacher who had told everybody?

Then, in afternoon break, Kimberley saw Paul Fox and understood. The police had told Kimberley that Paul had seen nothing, knew nothing of what had happened. But that wasn't the way he sounded when he was mouthing off to his mates.

"That Kimberley Pierce," he said loudly, as she and Cate crossed the corridor. "She's anybody's for a couple of cans of lager."

The other boys laughed.

"Busy tonight?" one asked her.

Something in Kimberley snapped. Before Cate

could restrain her, Kimberley ran into the gang of boys and began to pound her fists against Paul.

"Stop, stop, stop!"

The other boys stood back, waiting to hear what she said.

"I wasn't drunk," Kimberley shouted.

"That makes it better, does it?" Paul taunted. "Prak was all over you. If that other bloke hadn't come along you'd have done it with him, wouldn't you? You went with the other bloke 'cos he was older and bigger and then you got scared, called it rape. You weren't raped. You were asking for it!"

Kimberley began to hit him again. This time, Cate dragged her off. Paul was laughing his ugly little-boy laugh and his mates joined in. Kimberley had had enough. She turned and ran out of the school.

Jan and Clare were walking their beat at two-thirty. Clare had just been telling Jan about helping Ruth move rooms and how awkward she found it, not being able to tell Ruth about her partner's granddaughter. They had moved on to talking about the breakup with Neil when Clare spotted the girl they'd just been talking about. Kimberley Pierce was walking up the hill with her head on the shoulder of her best friend, Cate Connell. It looked like she was crying.

Clare got to her first.

"What's going on?" she asked.

"People at school, teasing her," Cate said.

These girls might be teenagers, but today they looked to her like frightened children. Clare put her arm around Kimberley.

"Tell me all about it," she said.

When Kimberley was done, Clare consulted Jan, then made a call to CID. Neil and Chris were out. Clare didn't want to waste time dictating a message to go on Dylan's pager. Finally, she managed to speak to their boss, DI Greasby.

"...from what this boy said to Kimberley half an hour ago, he saw the bloke who attacked her. My understanding was that, yesterday, the boy claimed not to have seen anything at all."

"Yes," Greasby said, "that's right. We'd better pick him up, question him again."

"School finishes in twenty minutes," Clare pointed out. "If we want to get hold of him, that's the one place we can be sure of finding him quickly."

"All right," Greasby said. "One of you take the girl home. The other go back to Greencoat, get the boy, and I'll meet you there."

Jan took Kimberley home while Clare hurried down to Greencoat. She got to the admin. office five minutes before the bell and asked to see the head. Maureen Bright was in a meeting, but the school secretary tracked down Paul Fox on a computerized timetable. One of the deputy heads hurried over and collected him.

"What's all this about?" the boy asked, when he and Clare were alone in the school's one interview room.

Clare got out her notebook. She wasn't meant to ask any questions, only to keep the boy until Greasby arrived. However, if he made any spontaneous admissions, she was going to make sure she took them down. She read the boy his rights, just to scare him.

"You lot have already spoken to me once," the boy complained.

"You haven't spoken to me," Clare said. "I know you. I know your type." She did, too. He was a lout and a loudmouth, thick as two short planks.

"I told them, I didn't see anything, all right?"

"Then you've been lying to somebody."

Clare looked at her watch. Outside, the school bell went. Where was Greasby?

"Who are we waiting for?"

"Someone more important than me," Clare said, in a quiet voice. Let him sweat.

"I'd rather talk to you," Paul said, as she'd hoped he would. It meant that he knew full well that he had held back evidence the day before.

"I'm listening," she said. "Do you want me to call your mother at work?"

"No!"

80

Clare made a note of this, then waited again. She wasn't going to question Fox, though he was old enough – he would leave school in a matter of days. But if he made a statement of his own free will... So far, all the police had was Kimberley's uncorroborated recollection. The only bit of the rapist which Prakesh saw clearly was his fist. Any kind of detailed description would be a godsend.

"The bloke who hit Prak," Paul Fox said, "the one who Kimberley reckons raped her – I've seen him around."

"Where? Who is he?"

"I didn't want to get involved."

"It's a bit late for that," Clare said. "What do you know about him?"

Paul hesitated, then spoke quietly. "His name's Smash. I don't know his real name. He was the one Kimberley went upstairs with. You won't tell him it was me who told you, will you?"

"Can you describe this *Smash* to me?"

"He's big. White. Wears a lot of rings. He's got shaved eyebrows. I dunno. Like I said, everybody knows who he is."

"Everybody? Why?"

"He's a dealer."

The door opened and DI Greasby walked in.

"This is Detective Inspector Greasby," Clare told Paul Fox. "He'll want you to tell him the things that you just volunteered to me. Can I have a word outside, sir?"

In the corridor, Greasby looked put out.

"You're not trained to ask questions, Constable."

"He knew what it was about, sir. He started talking. I could hardly stop him, could I? He's given me a name for the rapist. According to Fox, our man is a drug dealer, so there's a fair chance that we'll already have him on file."

"All right," Greasby said, trying hard not to look impressed. "Let's take him in and see what we can find."

Neil's shift was coming to an end. He had just returned to the office. A quick check told him that there had been no reports of anyone using Mark Brewer's stolen credit card. He and Chris had received no decent leads about the man who raped Kimberley Pierce, either. Neil picked up the phone to ring Wordsworth Hall and ask for a list of all their current and previous tenants. Then Clare Coppola walked into the room, accompanied by DI Greasby and Paul Fox. Greasby told Chris Dylan to put in a check for a known drug dealer who went under the alias, "Smash". Then he took Paul Fox to an interview room.

For a few seconds, Neil and Clare were standing by each other. They weren't alone in the room, but they were the only people without something to do.

"How come he told you when he wouldn't tell me and Chris?" Neil asked.

"He didn't tell me first. He told Kimberley – showing off." Clare gave Neil a sympathetic look.

"How are you?" she asked.

"All right. A bit tired. I put in a lot of overtime yesterday."

"Did you get anywhere with those burglaries before this case came along?"

Neil shook his head. "I was starting to, but then…"

Clare nodded. Both knew that a few petty burglaries were nothing when compared to rape, but it was frustrating not to be able to follow a case through.

"How are you?" Neil asked.

"Fine," Clare said with a wry smile. "We can still go out for a drink together, can't we?"

"Sure," Neil told her. "But you have to give me a little time first."

"Bingo!" Chris Dylan's voice called out, behind them.

They both went to join the sergeant. He read from a computer screen.

"Ashley Smith. Known alias: 'Smash'. Juvenile convictions for supplying crack cocaine. Nothing since, but he's been in court for rape and sexual assault. Acquitted both times. There's even an address."

"Current?"

"Only six months old." He smiled at Clare. "You've done a good job, Coppola. Want to come along for the climax?"

Clare winced at his choice of words, but said she'd go.

Neil and Dylan went in one car, she and Greasby in the other. The address they had was Hyson Green, on the edge of the red-light zone. They parked the unmarked cars a short distance from the house, half of whose windows were boarded up.

"Doesn't look promising," Greasby said. "You come to the front with me, Clare. Neil and Chris cover the back."

Greasby knocked on the door. Nothing. He knocked again. Clare was a little nervous. Footsteps came from the side of the house, shuffling through rubble. It was Neil.

"Any sign of life?" Greasby asked.

"No, sir. Looks like it's long abandoned."

Optimistically, Clare tried the door. It opened. A rat ran across the hallway. There was some mail scattered to the side of the door. Clare picked a few letters up. One of them was an electricity bill, addressed to a Mr A. Smith.

"He lives here."

"Or used to," Dylan said.

"Shall we have a look around?" Neil suggested.

"The front door was hanging open, right?" Dylan said.

"It looks abandoned to me," Greasby told him.

If the house was abandoned, they were within their rights to enter in order to effect an arrest. If it wasn't, and no one let them in, they would need to get a warrant from a magistrate, which would waste valuable time.

The house was on three floors. Neil took the ground floor, Greasby the first. Clare found herself following Dylan up to the third. Most of the doors were open. The rooms they passed had mattresses in them, and the debris from what happened on the mattresses.

"You know what this place is," Greasby said, as they pushed open the first closed door they came to. "A knocking shop."

A middle-aged man hurried out of the room, past Greasby, knocking Clare aside. Greasby charged down the stairs after him.

"Police, stop!"

Clare stood on the landing, alone. She walked into the bedroom, which was as desolate as the others. A girl sat on the bed, pulling on her tights. She was fifteen at the most.

"Hello," Clare said, in her friendliest voice. "I'm a police officer. Do you mind if I ask you a few questions?"

"Who gave you the right to barge in here?" the girl asked, in a thick Nottingham accent.

"The door was open."

"I'll bet."

Clare chose her words carefully. Downstairs, she could hear an altercation. The CID officers had grabbed the punter who was trying to escape.

"Look," Clare said, "I know you weren't doing anything illegal. I just want to ask you a few questions about someone who lives here."

It was true that the girl wasn't doing anything illegal. Prostitution itself was not a crime. Soliciting was. Loitering with intent to solicit was. But selling sex, the world's oldest profession, was not against the law.

"No one lives here," the girl said.

"What about the name on the bills downstairs."

"Bills? You think anyone pays the bills?"

Clare looked around. There was no bulb in the light fitting. The power was almost certainly cut off. She produced a photo from her notebook.

"Do you know this man?"

The girl looked at it. "Might."

"He's supposed to live here."

"Not any more, he doesn't."

"Do you know where I might find him?"

"Why? What's he done?"

Chris Dylan walked into the room. "All right, duck, get the rest of your clothes on. You're coming to the station with us. We've got a few questions for you to answer."

*　　*　　*

The girl, it transpired, was called Tracey Wicks. She had just turned fifteen. Tracey was meant to be living in a children's home nearby, but had absconded several times. The city had a large number of under-age prostitutes, most of whom should have been in care. Tracey wasn't unusual. From what they could tell, she lived in the Hyson Green house when she wasn't staying with a nineteen-year-old pimp who took most of her earnings.

Evidently the house where Smash used to live was condemned and due to become part of a car park. Ashley Smith had lived there until March and had used his name to get the power connected during the winter months, but the bill had never been paid. He had moved out when they were cut off. Tracey claimed not to know where he was. She might or might not be telling the truth.

The officers returned the girl to the home she had absconded from three months before, knowing full well that she would be off again, probably that very night. They let the middle-aged man they had caught her with go. He was an income tax inspector who was about to move to Nottingham with his family. He claimed that he was cruising the area looking for houses to buy, had come across Tracey and yielded to temptation. Of course, he had no idea that she was under-age, and prosecuting him wasn't worth the hassle. He had paid Tracey the price of a vial of crack cocaine. Sex with minors was cheap.

A second circular went out, this time giving the photo of Ashley "Smash" Smith, saying that he was "wanted for questioning concerning a serious sexual assault". However, at seven-thirty that Monday evening, no one had the least idea where he was.

By the time they knocked off at the same time on Tuesday evening, they were nowhere nearer finding him.

The squad worked until eight on Wednesday evening, but had no further leads. Smash Smith had gone to ground.

8

It was only the beginning of May, but the city was in the grip of a heatwave. Lorraine chose a thin, fifties-style cotton dress for the concert that Wednesday evening. She'd bought it second-hand from Pennyfeather's last term, but this was her first excuse to wear it. She'd been meaning to go with Sophie, but Sophie, only just back from a long weekend with her parents, said she didn't feel like it. Lorraine persuaded Melanie to buy Sophie's ticket off her. Melanie was dressed to kill, too. That night, the two girls walked into Rock City feeling like they were famous, clocking admiring glances from the boys they passed by.

Inside the hall though, it was swelteringly hot. The dress clung to Lorraine like clingfilm. When the band finally came on, she and Melanie joined the rush to the front. But the girls could only stand the throng for a few minutes. Bodies bashed against them, leaving bruises which would show for days. People were climbing on top of each other, trying to stage dive. They were clumsy drunks snatching a few moments of glory as they were bounced on shoulders to the front, before being grabbed by bouncers and dragged to the side. Worse, unseen hands groped Lorraine's body. Disgusting. She and Melanie pushed their way back out, finding a space at the side where they could just about see the show.

The singer was between numbers, sprinkling the steaming crowd with Evian water. When someone called out an insult, she challenged him to a fight. Half the audience hadn't come for the music. They'd come to gawp. But Lorraine loved the songs. And she loved the macho way the singer stood at the front, one leg raised, foot on the monitor. With her long blonde hair and low-cut pink dress, the singer looked like she was playing Blanche Dubois, the tarnished southern belle in a Tennessee Williams play Lorraine had done for A-level.

Lorraine's favourite part came towards the end, when the group did *Asking For It*. The singer put everything she had into the song, which was all about telling men where to get off. Lorraine was totally, totally involved in the gig. But then, just as the band were finishing their latest single, the hall plunged into blackness.

All of the venue's power had gone. The group left the stage. For a few minutes, the hall remained dark and eerily quiet. Then the emergency lights came on.

Lorraine wiped sweat from her brow. Then a guy was standing in front of her and Melanie. Lorraine didn't recognize him, but Melanie seemed to know who he was. While he was chatting her up, another guy came up to Lorraine. He was dark and heavy looking and Lorraine didn't fancy him, but she couldn't stop him talking to her.

"You look great tonight," he told Lorraine, eyeing her in the most obvious way. "I'd offer to buy you a drink but the beer pumps aren't working."

Lorraine gave him the brush off and went to the toilet. When she came back, Melanie and her friend were still in deep conversation. The power was back on but the band were packing up. Dance music had started in the disco downstairs.

"We're going to dance," Melanie told Lorraine. "Coming?"

"Better not. I've got a seminar first thing."

As the couple left, the dark guy was at Lorraine's side again.

"What about it?" he asked. "I'm a good dancer."

"Not tonight," she told him, trying to be nice about it. "I've got a seminar at nine and I need a shower before I go to bed."

"Maybe I could shower with you," he said, still smiling. Creep.

Lorraine shook her head. "Nice try. Good night."

The walk from Rock City to her hall of residence took a little over ten minutes. The evening had turned cooler and Lorraine enjoyed her stroll home. There were plenty of other people about, also returning from the concert, and she didn't feel vulnerable, the way she sometimes did in this city, late at night. Lorraine never took unnecessary risks. She wouldn't dream of cutting across the Forest, for instance, as some male students were doing. It might save her five minutes, but it was creepy, and bad things happened there. She was in a brilliant mood. Despite the early ending, it had been a great evening. Her ears were still ringing from the noise. Lorraine didn't hear footsteps, following her, as she turned on to Gregory Boulevard. She didn't hear anything. It was only when Lorraine was inside the building, at her own door, key turning in the lock — only then was she aware of someone behind her.

Before Lorraine could turn around or make a sound, she was being pushed into her room, in darkness. As Lorraine tried to scream, there was a hand around her mouth, and her face was being pushed on to the bed. A deep voice warned that if she looked round, or made a noise, he would kill her. She thought he meant it. Lorraine bit the pillow as he pulled her dress up.

Ruth Hunter and Roy Tate were at the edge of their beat, on the top of the hill where Forest Road meets Mansfield Road. On one side of them was Forest Fields. On the other, the city centre. They were driving towards Alfreton Road when the call came on the radio.

"Sexual assault. Wordsworth Hall."

"Where's Wordsworth Hall when it's at home?" Roy asked.

"I know it," Ruth said. "Gregory Boulevard."

The place was a big old building which had been converted into a hall of residence during one of the city's frequent student accommodation crises. Ruth often passed it when she was walking to Mapperley Park, where Ben had a flat. But she'd never needed to go in before.

Students gave the police little trouble. They were a law abiding lot, these days, for the most part. Statistically, drug offences apart, they committed far less crime than other people their age.

"That one."

Ruth and Roy drove into a courtyard and parked outside the building. It looked like they were first on the scene. The time was a little after midnight. There were still lights on in many of the rooms. As Roy got out, Ruth radioed to see if they had a room number for the victim. They hadn't. Then she followed Roy into the building.

Sexual assault is an intimate crime. If it comes to court, the victim is entitled to privacy. Ideally, she should also be entitled to privacy during the investigation. You didn't walk into a public place and start asking "Who's been raped?" in the same way you might ask "Who's been burgled?". But you had to ask questions. Chances were, by the following morning, half the hall would know who had been attacked and this knowledge would follow the victim around for the rest of her university career.

Ruth and Roy were aware of this, and tried to remain discreet. They stood in the foyer of the building, looking for any sign of the person who'd called them. A couple of students walked in and gave the police officers peevish, paranoid glances before going. A moment later, a young girl came running down the stairs.

"Did you call us?" Ruth asked.

The girl didn't reply directly.

"Third floor. She's completely out of it."

The victim sat in a corner of the room, her torn dress hitched up to reveal bruised skin, scratch marks. It was a very warm night, but she was shivering. Her eyes were unfocused, but not dilated. It looked like she was suffering from shock, not stoned.

"I found her a few minutes ago," the girl who'd brought the officers up said. "The door was open and she was ... just sitting there. She couldn't tell me what happened..."

"You did right to call us," Ruth said. "What's her name?"

"Lorraine. Lorraine Parker."

"Are you a friend of hers?"

"Sort of. I think she went out tonight with Melanie, down the corridor."

"Is Melanie in?"

"No. I checked."

"We're going to take Lorraine with us, get her examined by a doctor. Would you come with her?"

"I guess."

They put a blanket around Lorraine and walked her to the foyer. By now, the rumour machine was turned on and several doors opened. Students gathered in the foyer.

"Did anyone see anything?" Ruth asked, as they walked by. "Hear anything?"

All she got was blank faces.

Downstairs, more officers had arrived. Ruth told them the room number.

"The door's shut, but not locked. CID will want to close off the scene when they arrive. I don't suppose they'll get Scenes of Crime in until the morning. You'd better check if anyone saw anything."

Outside, Lorraine and her neighbour were in the back of the panda. Ruth's inspector arrived and had a quick word.

"Has she told you anything?"

"Hasn't opened her mouth."

"Well, try and ascertain that she was raped. We don't want to go in mob-handed if all she's done is had a row with her boyfriend. Meantime, there's a police surgeon on her way to Oxclose Lane."

Ruth went over to the car. She and Roy drove across the city at full pelt, siren blaring, getting to the far side of Sherwood within four minutes. She took Lorraine and her companion to the Victim Examination Suite. Rape statements were often traumatic and could take a long time. The suite, which everyone still called the Rape Suite, except when there was a victim within earshot, was at the far end of the station. It had two rooms. One had pictures on the wall, colourful IKEA sofas, a table with magazines and a small kitchen area. It was meant to be more private, and relaxing, than a standard interview room. The other room doubled as a surgery. It had a doctor's couch, a shower and a toilet.

Earlier in the week, Clare had taken a statement from a rape victim – some kid and a bloke she'd met at a party, Clare said. Ruth wondered what had actually happened to Lorraine, who was still in shock. She'd tried to ask, compassionately, but all she'd got out of Lorraine so far was "he wore a mask". That would make it a stranger rape, more serious in legal terms than what had happened to Clare's girl, and out of Ruth's league. That was a relief. She'd been trained to deal with rape victims, but Ruth had no desire to take Lorraine's statement.

Two officers from CID arrived and Roy briefed them.

"Think she was raped?" Ruth asked her partner, once they'd got back into the car and resumed their patrol.

"In a dress like that?" Roy replied, in a world-weary voice. "Looked to me like she was asking for it."

9

"I don't see that there's any connection between the two cases..." Dylan argued in the Incident Room on Thursday morning.

"All I'm saying is," Neil argued, "it's possible –"

"Case one," Dylan told him, "a thirteen-year-old girl is tricked into an isolated room by a twenty-two-year-old man and raped. Case two, a masked man either follows, or lies in wait for a student in her hall of residence, forces his way into the room and rapes her, using a condom."

"We don't know if Smash used a condom. Kimberley was too scared to notice. All we know is that he used to live nearby."

"We don't know for sure if case one was Smash, not until we find him and Kimberley identifies him."

"By the way," Inspector Greasby said, interrupting

the disagreement. "We finally tracked down the taxi driver who took Kimberley home on Saturday night. He has no recollection of Ashley Smith, or anyone else, putting Kimberley into his car. Said she seemed upset about something, didn't speak. We asked him how old he thought she was. You know what he said?"

"Sixteen," Neil guessed.

"Eighteen. Then he admitted that he didn't take a really good look at her. 'It was a busy night,' he said."

"I want to go to the hall of residence," Neil said. "I know the people there. This Lorraine who was raped gave me a really good description of the burglar."

"Now you think the burglar and the rapist could be the same person?"

"It's not impossible," Neil said.

Stranger rape was often accompanied by theft. Dylan looked at Greasby.

"We need some extra manpower," he said.

"I can pull in another aide."

"Two."

"All right. How about the officers who picked up the call last night?"

"I don't think we should use the bloke," Neil said. "He's Kimberley Pierce's grandfather."

Greasby raised an eyebrow. "I agree. What about the woman?"

"Ruth Clarke. She's a probationer."

"Good. A young woman will fit in better with the students you have to question. Now, how about someone from the other station?"

"Could I suggest Ben Shipman?" Neil said. "He's a very good –"

"I was thinking more of another woman," Greasby told him. "You got on well with the Coppola girl, didn't you, Chris?"

"She was very helpful with the arsonist last month."

Chris Dylan gave Neil a wary look. He knew that Neil went out with Clare, but not that they had just split up.

"She's caught up in the Kimberley Pierce case, already," Greasby said. "So involving her makes sense. I'll sort it out with their inspectors."

"Thank you, sir."

When DI Greasby had gone, Neil sighed.

"Not happy to be working with your girlfriend again?"

"She's not my girlfriend any more."

"Ah."

When Neil remained silent, Chris asked, "Who finished it? Her, or you?"

"You're always telling me not to ask stupid questions," Neil muttered.

"Do you want me to see the boss?" Dylan suggested, sympathetically. "Ask him to get someone else?"

Neil shook his head.

"Come on, let's get over to Wordsworth Hall."

Clare was woken by the telephone.

"For you," Sam called.

Clare sat on the stairs in her dressing-gown. It was Paul Grace.

"CID want you again. There's been another rape and they need some support with local knowledge. Are you up for it?"

"Am I?" Clare yawned. "I guess so."

"Don't sound so enthusiastic," Grace said, sardonically. "You're lucky we've got Gary, or I wouldn't be able to let you go. As it is, you're writing yourself a handy reference for transfer to CID in a year or two. And I'm the poor beggar who has to tell Jan Hunt that her shift's one short again."

"Sorry, sir. Thank you."

"That's the good news," Grace said. "Bad news is that they want you straight away. So get dressed and get over there."

"Sir."

As soon as Clare put the phone down, the damn thing rang again. It was Inspector Greasby.

"I'm on my way over, sir," she assured him.

"Good, but it's not you I want, it's PC Clarke. Do you two live together?"

"We lodge in the same house, yes."

"Get her for me, would you?"

"She's been on night duty, sir. She's only been in bed for a couple of hours."

"Tough. I'll let you break the news to her then. Tell her if she wants to work with us to get to the station by eleven."

Clare made a pot of tea and took it up to Ruth's attic room. It was bad enough having to work a nine to five when you'd only finished at ten the night before, but Ruth had finished at six in the morning. Why did they want her? Clare woke her friend gently and explained what was going on. Then they both got dressed and headed for the station.

"It's you," Melanie said, when she opened her door at nine-thirty. She looked wrecked. Neil had woken her up.

"How's Lorraine?" she asked.

"She's sedated," Neil told her. "Her parents are coming to pick her up this morning, take her home for a few days. We believe that you were out with her last night."

"Yes. I was. I just can't believe..." Her voice trailed off despairingly.

"It's urgent that we speak to you about anything you may have seen."

"I understand. But I didn't walk home with her. Look, give me a minute to get dressed, then I'll invite you in, OK?"

"Fine. Thanks."

Neil waited in the corridor. Further down it, yellow tape sealed off Lorraine Parker's room. Inside, Forensics were looking for evidence which would help pin-point the man who attacked her. Dylan came out of the room and joined him.

"Anything?" Neil asked.

Dylan shook his head. "It doesn't look hopeful."

Melanie opened the door. "Oh," she said. "There are two of you. I'm not sure that there's room for two people to sit down in here."

Neil and Chris exchanged glances. Neil was aware that he ought to back out, but he already knew Melanie. She might find it easier to talk to him.

"I think that we can both squeeze on to the bed," Dylan told Melanie.

Pale without her make-up, Melanie pulled the plastic chair from beneath her desk and turned round to face them.

"She went home without me," Melanie said, before they could ask any questions. "I wanted to stay and dance. She had a ... a seminar, I think it was, first thing."

"What time did you come home?" Dylan asked.

"I left Rock City just before it closed, at two. The first I knew about the attack was the yellow tape around Lorraine's room. Someone told me what happened." She tossed her hair back and looked at Neil. "I didn't sleep too well, as you can imagine."

"Did you see anything suspicious, anyone behaving oddly around you, or Lorraine?" Neil asked.

She shook her head.

"Lorraine told us that a man asked her to dance, while she was with you, and she turned him down. Do you remember this man?"

"I'm sorry, no."

"You'd just started talking to a man with short, black hair, who you later danced with. Does that help?"

"I'm sorry. All I remember is Lorraine wanting to go home straight away. She liked the band a lot, whereas I ... I'm more into dancing. Now I really wish I'd walked home with her..."

"The man you were talking to," Dylan said. "Could we have his name?"

"Why?"

"He might remember something," Neil said.

"Oh, yes, I'm sorry. It's Michael. I don't know his surname. He does psychology."

"Do you know where he lives?"

"No. Somewhere near here, I think. He walked me home."

She looked at Neil. "He's not my boyfriend or anything. He didn't come in. I can ask around, find out his address, if you like."

They asked a few questions about Lorraine, and her ex-boyfriends. Melanie said that Lorraine had plenty of boyfriends, but they never lasted long. Some stayed the night. Some didn't. Lorraine had never said anything about any of them being violent.

"But then she wouldn't, would she?"

Dylan looked at Neil, who shook his head.

"If you remember anything else, call," Neil said, handing her a card. "My home number's on the back," he added. "I'm just up the road."

"I remember. Thanks."

"She *remembers*?" Dylan said, when they were out of the room. "Fast work. How long ago did you split up with Clare anyway?"

"The weekend."

"You know, in CID, we have very strict rules about dating witnesses."

"Oh, yeah?" For a second, Neil thought the sergeant was being serious. Not that Neil was thinking about going out with Melanie Byatt. Not yet, anyway.

"Yeah, really. The rule is: senior officers get first crack."

Neil laughed, though he thought the joke was in bad taste. They knocked on the next door.

10

In the CID Incident Room, Detective Inspector Greasby brought Ruth and Clare up to date.

"Unfortunately," he concluded, "neither of the victims rate too highly on the sexual assault index."

"The *what*?" Clare asked.

"It's a list our research has come up with: the victim factors which help conviction."

There were five factors, Greasby explained:

1. The victim should be respectable.
2. She should be sexually inexperienced.
3. She should not have been raped by an acquaintance.
4. She should have fought and been hurt.
5. She should have reported the rape promptly.

Ruth thought that the list was sick. Rape was

rape. Why should any of these things make a difference to how the court saw it?

"Kimberley Pierce has factors one and two going for her," Greasby said.

"She didn't know the rapist," Clare protested.

"In a manner of speaking, no. But she went into a room with him. And she'd been drinking, which doesn't help. We tracked down the third boy she went to the party with – Darren Hicks – he's confirmed that the bloke she went off with was Smash, who he knew as a drug dealer. He also saw Smash putting Kimberley in a taxi. He says the guy had his arm around her and he assumed they'd just 'done it'. So the Crown Prosecution Service will call it an acquaintance rape, no matter what Kimberley thinks it was."

"And Lorraine Parker?" Ruth asked.

"She only has factor three going for her. The rapist wore a ski mask, she thinks. She was too frightened to get a good look."

"Why isn't she respectable?" Clare wanted to know.

"She's a student. She was wearing a dress which showed three inches of cleavage and she's had several sexual relationships in the past year. No judge is going to tell a jury that she's respectable."

"That's sexist garbage," Ruth argued. "You're not meant to be able to bring up a defendant's past sexual history in court. And what she was wearing has nothing to do with it. If she chose to walk the streets naked, it shouldn't make any difference."

Greasby gave Ruth a withering look.

"The defence always finds a way to introduce a woman's sexual history in court if it suits them. And judges comment on clothes, whether you like it or not. They're old guys. They have different standards."

And Roy Tate had commented on what Lorraine was wearing, Ruth remembered. That morning, Clare had told her how Kimberley was related to her partner. Ruth wondered when Roy would find out what had happened to his granddaughter.

"What about reporting it?" Clare asked. "Wasn't the attack on Lorraine Parker reported quickly?"

"It was," Ruth said, "but not by her. It was reported by another student on her corridor."

"All I'm trying to do," Greasby went on, "is to point out how difficult it is to convict men of rape, even when we catch them. For every ten rape complaints, there's one conviction. So we need to get as much evidence as possible. Now I want to use you two in Forest Fields. You know the area. You're the same age as the students we'll be dealing with. You should have a better chance of finding things out than some of my older officers."

"What about the man who attacked Kimberley Pierce?" Clare asked.

"We'll find him. It's only a matter of time. He

came here from Birmingham – that's where he got his first convictions. Best bet is he went back there. Brum CID are on the look out. But I very much doubt whether he's connected with the Lorraine Parker attack."

The Inspector was about to dismiss them when he remembered something.

"Oh, you should also be aware that there was a burglar making regular visits to Wordsworth Hall. Again, we're working on the assumption that the burglaries aren't connected with the attack on Lorraine Parker. Neil Foster has the details. A description's been circulated and is on the notice-board."

Ruth meant to look at the noticeboard, but she and Clare were distracted by the arrival of Chris Dylan.

"Any joy?" Greasby asked.

"Not really. Neil's trying to track down a student who might have seen the bloke who tried to pick up Lorraine. We've interviewed nearly everybody on her floor and some of the one above. By the time we got to the bottom two, most of the students were out. No one saw anything."

"Is it a mixed hall?" Clare asked.

"Yes," Dylan told her, "but the floors aren't. First and third, women. Second and fourth, men."

"Then what's to stop the rapist being someone who actually lives there?" Ruth suggested. "After all, he'd have no trouble getting in and escape would be easy. He'd just have to go up or down a floor."

"He'd also run a huge risk of being seen and recognized," Chris Dylan argued.

"Less than a complete stranger would. After all, he'd know the victim's movements. He'd know the times when the corridors are quiet. If he wore a mask over his head and didn't speak during the act, then took the mask off as soon as he got out of her room, it wouldn't even matter if anyone spotted him. He lives in the building. He's got a reason for being there."

"Ruth's right," Clare said. "One statistic you didn't throw at us earlier, Inspector. Seventy per cent of women are raped by someone they already know."

And, Ruth knew full well, two-thirds of acquaintance rapists got off.

"All right, all right," Greasby told them. "I never said that we were ruling anything out. But this place is easy to get into, as the number of burglaries proves."

"We're finding out where every man in the building was at the relevant time," Dylan added. "However, given that it was gone midnight, most of the ones we've seen so far claim to have been in bed. Only a couple of them have corroborating accounts from the people they were in bed with. I'll give you a list."

"Come on," Ruth said to Clare. "Let's get over there."

Neil knocked on the door of a shabby, three-storey house in Hyson Green. It took a while for anyone to answer. Eventually, a thin, long-haired youth in faded jeans came to the door. The time was eleven-thirty but it was clear that Neil had got him out of bed. Neil showed his badge.

"We're making a few enquiries. Is your name Michael?"

"No."

"Does someone called Michael live here?"

"Mike Hawkins. Yeah."

"Is he in?"

"Dunno."

"Perhaps you could take a look for me."

Students, Neil thought, as the boy ambled upstairs. Don't they have lectures to go to? After a while, another youth came down, wearing a towelling dressing-gown. He was tall, muscular, with a square, unshaven jaw. He was the sort of guy who Neil would imagine Melanie Byatt going out with.

"What do you want?" Hawkins asked, defensively.

"It's about something that happened last night," Neil said, "someone you might have seen. If I could have a couple of minutes of your time?"

"I'm not awake yet," Michael Hawkins said, showing Neil into a dusty living-room. "I had a late night. Let me get a drink. Want one?"

Neil waited while Michael Hawkins made them

both a mug of instant coffee. Then they sat down on sagging armchairs.

"Last night, you were with a girl called Melanie Byatt," Neil began.

"That's right," Hawkins said. "I danced with her for an hour or so, after the gig."

"You were with her until...?"

"Just gone two. I walked her home, then came back here."

"You didn't go into Wordsworth Hall?"

"No. I saw her to the door. She didn't ask me in."

Satisfied, Neil moved backwards. "At Rock City, do you remember that Melanie was with a friend?"

"Yeah. She introduced me. I don't remember her name."

"Lorraine. She was wearing a low-cut pink dress."

Hawkins nodded. "Yeah. You couldn't miss her."

"But you didn't talk to her."

"Nah. She wasn't really my type. Too obvious. Anyway, I'd already connected with Melanie. What's all this about?"

"I'll come to that in a moment. I'd like you to think carefully, Michael. Do you remember anyone talking to Lorraine?"

"No. Why should I? I was with Melanie."

"When you were with Melanie, do you remember anyone asking Lorraine to dance?"

"I was pretty focused on Melanie. Nah, wait. There was someone..."

Neil waited silently.

"I can't remember what he was wearing," Michael began, "but I'd recognize him again. I know I've seen him around."

"Where?"

"Trent University. Rock City, too, maybe. I go there a lot. This guy, what's he done?"

"Nothing, probably," Neil said. "But we need to eliminate him from our enquiries. Could you describe him for me?"

"Smaller than me – five-eight, five-nine maybe. Five-ten at the most. Dark hair, cut really short. Not stocky, but built ... if you know what I mean."

"Age?"

"Between nineteen and twenty-three."

He could, Neil realized, be describing Ashley Smith. He got the photo out of his pocket. Lorraine hadn't been shown this photo yet.

"Would this be the guy?"

Michael Hawkins took one glance at the photo and shook his head. "Nothing like."

"Would you be willing to go through some photographs of current students," Neil asked, "maybe help put together a photofit picture?"

"Only if you tell me what this is about."

Neil told him.

Kimberley got out of bed just after eleven. This was her third day off school. The counsellor she'd spoken to had suggested that she stay away until next week. Hopefully, by then, the police would have captured the man who'd raped her. They knew who he was now. Inspector Greasby had been round and shown Kimberley a photograph. She'd said yes, it was him. She hadn't asked his name, didn't want to know his name, not yet.

Downstairs, the doorbell rang. Kimberley looked at the Victim Support leaflet which Clare Coppola had given her. She reread the sections headed "Feelings" and "Family and Friends". The phrases cut through her thoughts like a scalpel.

Reactions include shock or disbelief, and feelings of degradation and humiliation. Some people wrongly blame themselves. Others feel numb initially, and emotions may take some time to surface ... those close to you also experience shock. They too are often confused, feel inadequate and unsure how to help or cope with the situation. They can best help by: Being prepared to listen; Accepting your feelings; Giving practical support and encouragement.

Mum knocked on Kimberley's door.

"It's Grandma, love. Maybe best if you stay in your room until she's ready to come up and see you."

Kimberley nodded. Grandad was on nights this week and Mum had asked her to come while he was sleeping. She wanted to tell her what had happened before Grandad heard it from somewhere else.

Grandma would be very upset, Mum had warned. Kimberley could understand why Mum was worried about Grandma's reaction. For Kimberley was always on best behaviour when her grandparents were around. To them, she was innocent, still a child, really. It would hurt them to know that someone had ... that someone had...

But didn't Mum realize how that made Kimberley feel? It made her feel guilty for upsetting Grandma. Guilty for going to the party which – all right, yes, she knew – she should never have gone to. Guilty because a man much stronger than her had thrown her to the ground, and, and...

He'd done it before, DS Dylan had told Kimberley, to women older than her. As if that would make her feel better, feel it wasn't her fault. He'd raped one, and another had fought him off. But, both times, he'd been acquitted. The jury didn't believe the woman. This time, hopefully, he'd be convicted. Hopefully. Kimberley couldn't understand how there could be any doubt about it.

She went and sat on the edge of the stairs, listening to the conversation.

"Why are you off work?" Grandma was asking.

"To look after Kimberley."

"Is she ill? You should have called me earlier. You can't afford to lose a day's pay."

"She's not ill, not exactly. Something ... happened, on Saturday night." Kimberley listened to Mum telling the story. She listened to the silences where Grandma must be crying. She listened to the words which people tried to use lightly when they were saying them to her. "Test. Negative. But then she has to take another one in three months. We won't really know until then."

By listening, Kimberley hoped to make sense of what had happened, to work out what it meant to her. But she only felt more confused. After a while, Grandma told Mum she'd like to go upstairs and see her. Kimberley tiptoed back into her room, with its cuddly toys and pop group posters. She pretended to be reading a book about ballerinas.

"Kimberley?"

Then Grandma was holding her in her arms, saying, "I'm so sorry. I'm so sorry."

Kimberley said nothing. What was she supposed to say? *You should let it all out*, the counsellor had told her, but who really wanted to hear? Cate, yes. The girls at school, but only for the gossip. Mum, because she felt she had to. But no one wanted to hear what it was really like to lose control of your body, to have someone hurt you that way, there. How would they know? Why would they want to know?

"Oh, Kimberley," Grandma said. "How am I going to tell your grandad?"

11

The city has two universities. The older one is based entirely on a campus, next to Wollaton Park. There are a dozen or so halls of residence on the site. The thief doesn't know his way around them, though he's heard the security is lax. He'll do them, but not yet. When he burgles a place, he needs to look as though he belongs, knows where he's going. So maybe he'll pick up a student who can show him around. He'll wait for the new crop in the autumn.

The newer university also has a campus site, further out of the city, on the edge of a vast council estate called Clifton. It has plenty of small halls of residence, and the thief knows them well. Although he's always lived in Forest Fields, he's visited friends in hall. He's even stayed the night, more than once. The rooms have better locks than those in Wordsworth Hall. This afternoon he needed to use a big screwdriver to prise the doors open. But it was worth it. He got a good haul: a cheque book with its accompanying card, two cameras, an electronic organizer, some cash, a large lump of dope and a CD Walkman.

Knowing when to stop is the secret. Hang around too long and you're sure to be noticed. Ironically, the only time that anyone's spotted him, spoken to him, was when he wasn't thieving at all. It was last Friday night, when he went to see the raped girl, Sophie, to check how she was.

The secret is not to be greedy. He only goes out thieving once, or, at the most, twice a week. Once a week he works in a shelter for the homeless. The rest of the time he sees friends. He's doing an acting class. He's not sure if he's any good at acting, but it's a laugh. You get to meet a lot of women, too.

On his way out of the campus, walking to the bus stop, the thief is tempted to steal a car. How come so many undergraduates have cars and he doesn't? Their parents must have money to throw away. Theoretically, the thief knows how to get into a car and start it, but he knows better than to try, especially since he has a bag full of stolen property under his arm. The thief waits in line with the other students to take the bus into town.

The thief considers using the cheque book straight away. The sooner he uses it, the better. Its loss will be reported and the information circulated within twenty-four hours. But he needs time to practise the signature on the card. And he needs to work out which banks he hasn't been to, first checking that they don't have video cameras recording every transaction. It's getting to the point where it's safest to stick to shops. But shops don't sell money and his flat is already full of luxury goods. If the thief buys stuff to sell on, he's lucky to get a third of what it costs.

Maybe he'll go straight to the library when he gets into town. They have those private study booths there, where he can perfect his new signature securely. Thinking about these things, the thief doesn't notice the guy who joins the queue two people behind him. It's only when the bloke is getting on to the bus that the thief gets a brief look at his face. Even then, the thief isn't sure. He sits near the guy and, for a moment, their eyes meet. The other man gives no hint of recognition, but the thief is sure.

Sitting opposite him is the man he saw leaving Sophie's room, six days ago. The man who raped her.

For the rest of the bus journey, the thief thinks long and hard. What should he do? The thief memorizes every feature of the rapist's face. He notes what he is wearing. The man must be a student, so the thief tries to make out the name of a book poking out of his bag, to see if he can tell what course he's on. The man might live on the Clifton site, or maybe he just does a course which runs there. If the thief follows him when he gets off the bus, he could find out where he goes, and work it out.

But. It's the same "but" as before. Even if he finds out, who does he tell? There must be a way to inform the police anonymously, but why would they take him seriously? He might easily be someone with a grudge, looking to get even with the guy. No. The police would need a witness statement. And if he gave a statement, he would have to explain what he was doing in Wordsworth Hall last Friday afternoon. Moreover, as far as the thief knows, Sophie hasn't reported the rape. So why should he get involved?

The bus stops in the city centre. The rapist gets off. The thief gets off. He starts to follow him. The rapist stops outside Debenham's, buys a local paper from a street vendor. The thief reads the headline on the vendor's poster: *GIRL'S RAPE NIGHT-MARE IN CITY HALL OF RESIDENCE.* So Sophie must have reported it in the end. Good. The thief follows the rapist up the hill, past Selectadisc, keeping a careful distance. As they cross Lower Parliament Street, the rapist makes the pedestrian lights. The thief doesn't. He has to jog to catch up when the lights change again.

The thief passes the Royal Concert Hall. He can see the rapist further up Goldsmith Street. He passes Chaucer Street. The thief walks quickly, trying not to draw attention to himself. The rapist doesn't look round. He turns right on to Shakespeare Street, where most of the university buildings are. The thief runs to catch him up. Turning the corner, he's just in time to see the rapist going into the student union building. This doesn't tell the thief anything, except that the guy's a student, which he's already worked out. The thief follows him inside, but can't find him.

The thief wastes five minutes looking around, then realizes that he's getting suspicious looks himself. Moreover, he's carrying a bag full of stolen goods. It's time to give up. The thief buys a local paper and reads it on the way home.

Neil went home for his lunch. He would be working late tonight and he was already frazzled, needed a breather. The only way to make sure he got a lunch hour was to leave the station. He'd put the kettle on and was making himself a ham and tomato sandwich when the doorbell rang. He nearly didn't answer it. However, when he got to the door, Neil was glad that he had.

"Hi. I got a message that you wanted to see me. When I rang they said you were home, so ... I hope you don't mind."

Melanie Byatt looked as lovely in jeans and a T-shirt as she did in a dress the other night. Neil congratulated himself on having given her his address.

"Come in," he said. "I was just making myself some lunch. Have you...?"

"Oh, I'm fine."

She followed him into the kitchen. The kettle clicked off.

"Can I offer you a cup of tea, at least?"

"That'd be nice. Actually..." she admitted. "That sandwich does look good."

Neil smiled, feeling like his mother, happy only when she was feeding people.

"I'll make you one too."

As he was cutting more bread, Neil explained why he wanted to see her.

"It's just that your friend Michael remembered the guy and I wondered if I described him to you, it might ring a bell. We've got Michael looking at some photos tomorrow, and two heads are better than one, that kind of thing."

"I'll try," Melanie said.

He told her what Michael Hawkins had told him. She shook her head.

"Sorry. I really wasn't looking."

"Too interested in Michael?" he asked, without turning round.

She didn't reply until he handed her the

sandwich. He thought that she was going to tell him that it was none of his business. She didn't.

"I thought I might be," she said. "But, later, I decided I wasn't."

"Your girlfriend?" she asked, as they walked into the living-room. She was pointing at the picture of Clare on the mantelpiece.

"Ex-girlfriend."

"Most people don't keep photos of their ex's on display."

"We only split up at the weekend," Neil told her. "I haven't got around to it yet."

"I'm sorry," she said. "What happened?"

Neil tried to think of some macho, understated way of explaining that he and Clare were mutually incompatible. He couldn't do it. Instead, he found himself telling Melanie the story of his relationship with Clare. It was the first time he'd really talked about it when he was sober. She listened intently, eating her sandwich.

"I was kidding myself," he finished, "all the time, those two years. We were friends who really liked each other, but there was always something missing."

"What?" Melanie asked.

"It's hard to explain. No. I think ... I was kind of obsessed with her, but I could never fully relax when I was with her. She didn't love me, or ... not enough ... and I was always wanting to convince her, which made things worse, because I was on edge a lot of the time. Does that make sense?"

"Perfect sense," Melanie said. "I had a relationship like that once. Mind you, it lasted two months, not two years."

"Two months is probably all we should have lasted," Neil said, wryly. He looked at his watch. His hour was nearly over.

"I ought to go," Melanie said. "I'm making you late. You haven't even started your sandwich yet."

"You're easy to talk to," Neil said. "I hadn't realized how long…"

She smiled and stood up. "Maybe we can talk again," she said. "Thanks for the sandwich. Enjoy yours."

Neil stood too. The timing was all wrong, he knew that, but he wasn't sure when he'd get another chance like this, not with Melanie on her own.

"Maybe we could … go out," he said. "For a drink or…"

"I'd like that," Melanie said. She gave him her silly smile. He guessed it meant that she was nervous too.

"I'd say this weekend, only I won't know what overtime they're putting me on until tomorrow."

"I understand," she told him. "Call me any time. I'm not far away."

He opened the door for her. "Thanks for coming."

"Call me," she repeated, and kissed him on the cheek.

Neil went back into the living-room in a kind of daze. The last thing on his mind had been to start another relationship, yet... Without really thinking about what he was doing, he took Clare's photograph from the mantelpiece and put it in a drawer.

"Why aren't you at Wordsworth Hall with Clare?" Dylan asked Ruth on Thursday afternoon.

"We agreed it would be more effective to go at different times," she explained. "We'd catch more people in that way. Inspector Greasby said..."

"All right, all right."

Now that they were dealing with two cases, DI Greasby was making more of the decisions. Dylan didn't like it.

"Where is the boss?" he asked.

"In court," Tracey told him. "The armed robbery trial. Should be back soon."

Dylan started to say something but stopped as the office door crashed open, then slammed shut. A red-faced Roy Tate walked to the centre of the room. He was wearing civilian clothes. And he was shouting.

"Why didn't you tell me? My own granddaughter! Why didn't anyone tell me?" He was staring at Ruth.

"I only found out this morning," she stammered. "I'm so sorry, Roy. I..." But Roy was already confronting Dylan.

"Saturday night. Five days ago. What were you

waiting for? So I could read it in the paper?"

"We kept it out of the paper," Chris said, quietly. "It was up to your daughter, Karen. She didn't want you to know at first. She thought it would put more pressure on Kimberley. Something like that."

Roy swore. Ruth had never seen him like this before. Normally he was mild mannered, a friendly community copper. But it was all a front, she saw that now. Inside, he was just as angry as everybody else. Today, he was mad.

"She didn't want me to know because she knew I'd blame her. You know what she told me on Saturday? She said Kimberley couldn't see me on my birthday because her father had shown up out of the blue and insisted on taking her out. She lied to me so that my grandkid could go and get, and get…"

"We're doing everything we can, Roy," Ruth said, gently. "We know who it is. It's only a matter of time before…"

"Oh, no," Roy said. "I know the system. Just give me the evil bastard's name. I'm due for retirement. I'll take my chance in court. Just give me the bastard's name, so I can make sure he never gets to do this to anyone again!"

Wordsworth Hall had forty-four rooms, eleven on each floor. Nine of the students on Lorraine Parker's floor had been interviewed so far during the day, all but Janice Cole and Sophie Turner, who were still out when Clare knocked on their doors for a second time in the late afternoon. Now she had to work her way through the other three floors. Clare decided to start at the top.

The first person who answered was a smartly-dressed boy with a Birmingham accent. Clare introduced herself.

"I'm Mark Brewer. So you've found him, have you?"

"Sorry?"

"The man who nicked my credit card. Do you know how much he took on it? Four hundred and thirty-two pounds, seventeen pence, that's how much."

"No. I'm sorry," Clare said. "It's not about that. Were you in your room last night, just after midnight?"

"Yes, of course I was – asleep. Why? Has he been again?"

"No. Something happened. We don't think it's connected with the recent burglaries. I wonder, did you hear anything around that time, anything at all … unusual?"

"I told you, I was asleep. I never stay awake beyond half eleven. I'd go to bed earlier, but it's too noisy round here until then."

Clare thanked him and went to the next room. Twenty minutes later she had found five people in and learned nothing whatsoever. Still, the fourth floor was always going to be the least promising. She moved down to the second.

If the theory which Ruth had floated this morning was to prove true, the rapist had to live on the fourth or second floor. Lorraine had been able to tell the police nothing about him, except that he used a condom and wore a back to front ski mask with crudely cut out eyes. These details were so sketchy that Clare could almost believe Lorraine was making them up, that the rapist was someone she knew and Lorraine was protecting him. But Ruth had got there first and Ruth believed her. Clare trusted Ruth's instincts.

The next student to open his door was called Chris Williams. He looked young for a student, or maybe it was just that students looked younger to Clare these days.

"Come in," he said. "I like a woman in uniform."

She gave him her *no chance, mate* look and questioned him in the doorway.

"I need to ask where you were between midnight and twelve-thirty last night."

"Right here," Chris told her, "in bed. No late nights for me. I study law. There are lectures at nine every day."

"I wonder, did you hear any sounds, anything at all unusual at around that time?"

He shook his head.

"This is about the poor girl who got raped, right?

I was fast asleep at the time. I wish I'd heard something, but the truth is, I sleep really heavily."

"OK," Clare said. "Thanks for your time."

There was a girl walking up the stairs who Clare didn't recognize. It was possible that Neil and Chris had interviewed her earlier, but Clare checked her name anyway.

"Sophie Turner."

"I've been trying to see you, Sophie. Could I come up to your room? Have a brief chat."

"I don't know anything," Sophie said. "Can't we talk here?"

"I guess," Clare told her. "Do you know what this is about?"

Sophie nodded. She looked like the nervous type, Clare thought, the sort of girl who wanted to stay in hall for all three years of her degree course. Only there were never enough places.

"I was in bed," Sophie said. "I didn't see anything."

"Perhaps you heard something," Clare said. "It happened on your corridor, just after midnight."

"Where's Lorraine?" Sophie asked.

"She's gone to her parents for a couple of days, to get over it."

"You think it'll only take a couple of days?" Sophie said, sarcastically.

"No," Clare told her. "I didn't mean to sound callous."

She was about to let the girl go. Sophie had nothing to tell her. But there was something about the girl. She was scared.

"Look," Clare told her. "I know that this is very upsetting, but the … the attacker is very unlikely to come again. My inspector's talked to the warden. The outside door lock is being changed tomorrow. They'll be installing new locks on your room doors and video surveillance over the summer. What's happened to Lorraine is horrible but…"

A boy walked past them up the stairs. Another one Clare hadn't spoken to.

"I wanted to be in a single sex hall," Sophie said. "Lots of girls do. But the university says that boys don't like them."

"No," Clare said, "I don't suppose they do."

"Can I go now?"

"Uh, yes, thanks for your time."

Sophie left. She was spooked, Clare realized. It was a natural reaction. Tonight, she wouldn't much feel like sleeping in Wordsworth Hall herself.

12

On Friday morning, Sam stood outside Marks and Spencer's, clipboard in hand, looking for professional women in the twenty-five to thirty-four age group. Women her own age, in other words, only she didn't think of herself as professional. Sam was married at twenty, divorced at twenty-five. She'd kept the house, but the mortgage had twenty years to go and she could only afford to pay it by taking lodgers. She'd been able to get nothing beyond low paid, part-time work. This was the best job she had ever had, and it was boring. What made it worse was people walking down the street saw you standing there, trying to catch their eye, and did a detour to avoid being bugged. And even worse than them were the ones who, once stopped, wouldn't stop talking.

She nearly had her quota for the day. Sam had to persuade one more professional woman aged between twenty-five and thirty-four to discuss how she felt about banks and building societies. It was tempting to make one up, fill in the answers herself, but the company did random checks, and she couldn't afford to lose the job. The money from the two rooms she rented out barely covered the mortgage.

The weather had turned again. It was impossible to predict how a day was going to be when you left the house in the morning. Then, the sky was blue. By midday it could be sweltering or cold, with sudden showers. Now it began to rain, and Sam didn't have a coat with her, only a cardigan, which she needed to put on because her top was sleeveless, and she was shivering. As Sam reached into her bag, a warm hand gripped her bare shoulder.

"You look cold."

Sam looked up to see Steve, in his familiar old leather jacket, giving her his best smile.

"I was just getting my cardi out."

"Here." He whipped off the jacket and draped it round her shoulders.

"There's no need..."

"Let me buy you a drink."

Sam didn't argue. They walked up to the Royal Children, where Steve pulled out a wallet which was unusually full. Sam didn't want to ask where

Steve got the money. Last time they spoke he'd sworn that he'd packed in stealing.

"How's it going?"

"All right," Sam said.

"Still getting on with your lodgers?"

"Yes," Sam assured him.

"You don't sound too convincing."

Steve didn't like the fact that she lived with two police officers.

"Well, the atmosphere in the house is a bit heavy at the moment. They're both working on rape cases. You must have read about them."

Steve frowned. "I only read about one, just down the road from you, on Wednesday night."

"There was another at the weekend. A thirteen-year-old girl. Her grandfather's a policeman."

Steve looked guilty.

"What's on your mind?" she said.

His look changed. "You are. I miss you."

"Don't start that."

Steve was very good-looking, and charming, when he wanted to be. But he was also a big, selfish baby, who couldn't commit himself to a woman for more than a few weeks. She and Steve had had their few weeks last year, when he was at a loose end after graduating, and she was hard up for affection. She was hard up again, but didn't want to make the same mistake twice.

"There's something else," she said. "I can tell."

"You know," Steve said. "You're the only person in this city who really knows me."

"That's because we lived in the same house for the best part of two years. What is it? Have you been caught again?"

She knew that Steve had a suspended sentence. If he was found guilty of another imprisonable criminal offence, that would be it, he'd go to jail.

"No. But it's connected with that."

"Well...?"

Steve scrunched up his eyes the way he did when he was concentrating.

"Can we talk about it somewhere private?" he said. "Your place?"

"Why not yours?" Sam suggested. "Clare and Ruth come in at odd times. I don't want..."

This wasn't strictly true. But there was no need to tell Steve that both girls were working a nine to five this week. Sam didn't want the neighbours to see her ex-lodger visiting her house. Not after what he'd done to them. And, anyway, she was curious to see where he was living.

"All right," Steve told her. "I'll give you the address." He wrote it down. He was living in a flat only five streets from Sam's.

"I've got a couple of things to do, first," Steve told her. "I'll be home in an hour. If you want to come by any time after that..."

"All right," Sam told him. "I'll be there."

She finished her drink and went back outside, where the sun was shining and office workers were coming to the end of their lunch hour. There was a woman in a smart two-piece lingering outside Dawson's Bakery. She looked at least thirty. Sam hoped she wouldn't lie about her age.

"Excuse me," she said, in her smarmiest voice, "could you spare five minutes of your time?"

Clare checked in to the station at two. She'd spent all morning doing a door to door in the Meadows, asking after Ashley Smith. She'd come across several people who knew him, but none who'd seen him since the weekend. Nor had she found anyone who would admit to being at the party where the man raped Kimberley Pierce. "Smash", she discovered, was widely known for dealing in the less glamorous drugs: speed, jellies and crack cocaine. Most of the people she interviewed assumed that Clare was from the Drugs Squad.

"Where's Chris?" she asked Neil, who was hunched over a computer screen. The two of them had barely exchanged a civil word all week.

"He's with Michael Hawkins at the university, going over photos of all their students to see if he can pick out the one who tried to chat Lorraine up on Wednesday night."

"A bit of a long shot, don't you think? What are you up to?"

Neil pointed at the screen. "These have just come in. Criminal records of past and present residents of Wordsworth Hall. Only a handful of names. Any of them mean anything to you?"

Clare took a look. "No. Do any look promising?"

"Two possessions. One shoplifting. A cheque fraud and an indecent exposure."

"What about that last one?" Clare suggested.

"Yeah. Except that he's returned to New Zealand. I was thinking the cheque fraud might be our burglar. Bloke called Maurice Brennan. Still lives in Hyson Green."

"Want to go and see him?"

"I guess. Only trouble is, his photo's nothing like the description we've got."

"I haven't seen the description," Clare said.

"Well, you should have. It's on the noticeboard."

Clare went over to the board and found the sheet Neil was referring to. It contained a precise description of Steve Garrett, who she used to share a house with.

"Is this a possible," she asked Neil, "or is this definitely the guy we're after?"

"Oh, it's definitely him," Neil replied. "We've got three independent witnesses, all giving the same description. One of them's Lorraine Parker. We're not ruling out that he might be the man who raped her."

"Only…"

Neil caught the tone in her voice and stood up. "What?"

"The physical description exactly matches the guy who used to live in our house – Steve. I'm amazed you didn't notice that."

Neil looked annoyed. "I only met the guy once, as I recall."

"He has a leather jacket, just like the one described here."

"Really? He didn't wear it to the theatre."

Clare remembered their meeting now – Steve came to a musical at the Theatre Royal. Neil had been jealous because he could tell Clare was attracted to him.

"What's his surname?" Neil asked.

"Garrett."

"Let's look him up."

Neil went to the computer. "Gotcha! He lived in Wordsworth Hall the year it opened, three years ago, his first year at university. Hold on, though. He's got a criminal record, hasn't he? Why didn't that come up?"

"He was only convicted on Monday," Clare said. "It won't be on the computer yet."

"Know where he lives now?" Neil asked.

"No. But he's around."

"Would Sam know? For forwarding mail, that kind of thing."

"I don't think she does. He doesn't get much

mail. His dole cheque doesn't come to the house, I know that."

Neil did a PNC check. Steve's conviction might not be on the computer yet, but his latest known address would. A minute later, he put the phone down.

"According to our records, loverboy still shares a house with you."

"Neat," Clare said. "He seems to have done as good a disappearing act as Smash. I'll ask around, see if I can find out where he is now." She looked at her watch. "I'm going to join Ruth."

Her friend was doing a door to door in Forest Fields with Chris Dylan.

"Want me to look up this Maurice Brennan while I'm out?" she asked Neil.

"Can't hurt. But check with Chris first."

Neil gave her the details. Clare thought about asking to borrow his car, but then remembered she wasn't his girlfriend any more. She'd take the bus.

As the 91 rolled down Mansfield Road, she thought about Steve. She could see him burgling the hall of residence – if he still had a key from his days there, they were easy pickings. But could he be the rapist, too? Steve was the sort of guy who had no trouble getting girlfriends, but that didn't necessarily mean anything. And there were times, when Clare was alone in the house with him, that she had felt uneasy. It was something about his manner. He was predatory, ready to pounce if she showed him the smallest way in.

No, she was being silly. All that meant was that he fancied her and showed it. What made Clare uneasy was that she fancied him, too. If he hadn't spent so much time undressing her with his eyes she might have given him a chance. Until, that is, she'd realized that he was a criminal.

Ruth was doing a door to door of Forest Fields on her own. She was meant to be with Dylan, but he was busy. The Lorraine Parker investigation was going nowhere fast. Several students had been up the night before. A couple of them returned to the building within minutes of the attack. None of them, with the exception of the girl who reported the rape, had seen or heard anything.

Ruth's shift sergeant wanted her back. CID might be understaffed, but so was he. That morning, DI Greasby had told Ruth that she could expect to rejoin her shift for the weekend, which meant her working tonight and Saturday night. It was hardly fair, but at least she would get her rest days on Monday and Tuesday – if, that was, CID didn't call her in.

Unlike Clare, Ruth had no great yearning to join CID, and doing this door to door confirmed her feelings. It was routine, boring work. Ruth would rather be on foot patrol.

"Anything?" Clare asked, as they met up in the street.

Ruth shook her head. "Are you relieving Chris?"

"That's up to him. There's someone who showed up on Neil's computer check – a Maurice Brennan – who we have to check out, a possible burglar."

"Why are we wasting time on the burglar?"

"Actually," Clare said. "I think I've worked out who the burglar is."

"Who? How?"

Clare showed her a photocopied description. "Ring any bells?"

Ruth knew what she was getting at.

"All right, it sounds like Steve. But there are loads of people who look like that round here."

"Loads?"

"Maybe I'm exaggerating. But surely he wouldn't be stupid enough to… You don't want to arrest him again, do you?"

"I think we'll let someone else bring him in," Clare said. "That is, presuming they can find him."

Maurice Brennan wasn't in. Ruth and Clare were about to resume their door to door when a message came in on Ruth's pager. Ruth had never used one before. It was a small grey vodapager, with a tiny screen which could display up to 40 pages of text. The message had only two pages. The first one read as follows:

MICHAEL HAWKINS HAS
IDENTIFIED OUR BOY AS
ONE CRAIG SWIFT, A
SECOND YEAR ENGINEERING
STUDENT. HE SHOULD BE
LEAVING A LECTURE AT...

The second page told Ruth the location and asked her to meet Dylan there in fifteen minutes. They would be pushed to make it.

"Coming?" she asked Clare.

"Try and stop me."

They ran back to the house to pick up Ruth's car.

Sometimes, Steve felt like he was two people. There was the thief, the guy who got away with things, whose booty filled this grubby flat. Then there was Steve, who also lived here, who had a mediocre degree, no job and a brand new criminal record. Steve was busy tidying the flat so that Sam wouldn't notice some of his newest acquisitions. He shoved the computer games he had bought that morning under his bed, along with the stolen Megadrive which he'd been looking forward to playing them on. He put the new clothes which he had bought with the stolen credit cards out of the way. He hid bottles of expensive spirits.

It was silly, really, hiding the stuff, because, when Sam came round, he had to tell her what he'd been up to. How else could he explain his dilemma? Would she sympathize? Steve didn't know. He didn't know how she felt about him any more. For a few months, or maybe it was only weeks, they had been lovers. But then something went wrong. He didn't know what. Maybe she grew a little too needy, a little too real. They got so close that, at times, she reminded him of his mother. Or maybe he had his eye on someone else. They'd been keeping it quiet, because Sam didn't want the other students in the house to know that they were getting it on. He'd started sleeping in his own bedroom for more of the time until, slowly, without even speaking about it, they'd split up.

The doorbell rang and he went down to answer it. Sam had changed into casual clothes. She had fresh make-up and lipstick on, too, and he wondered for a moment whether she had made the effort for him or for herself.

"Big house," was all she said as she followed him up the stairs.

"I've got the top floor."

"I hope there isn't an attic."

"No."

She looked around his dingy flat. "You've made an effort to brighten it up, I guess."

"Drink?"

He realized that he'd hidden half the best drinks.

"Tea, if you've got it."

When he came back from his tiny kitchen with the drinks, she was looking at the boxed CD set he'd bought with Mark Brewer's credit card.

"Had a birthday, have you?"

She knew when his birthday was.

"Not exactly."

Then he told her about his visits to Wordsworth Hall, concluding on Friday afternoon, a week ago. He told her about Sophie.

"As soon I got into the room, it was obvious what had happened. When I could get some sense out of her, it seems she was coming back from having a shower. He pushed his way into the room, with a ski mask over his head. He raped her. I told her to report it, but she didn't want to. She said she'd never be able to live with everyone knowing and, anyway, rapists never went to prison. What she'd been through was bad enough without a trial on top of it."

"So what did you do?" Sam asked.

"I stayed with her a couple of hours. She wouldn't let me get anyone else. Then I went home. The next day, I went to see her again, but she wasn't there. Someone told me that she'd gone to stay with her parents. That's it. I haven't been back. I think I would have left it there, only, yesterday, I heard about the second rape. Not only that, but I saw the guy who did it. He's a student."

Sam's jaw dropped. Steve gave her a minute to take it in, then asked: "What should I do?"

143

"Two for the price of one?" Dylan said.

Clare knew that he was teasing her for turning up, but it was Ruth who replied.

"Actually, I'm supposed to have gone off duty, because I'm on nights tomorrow and Saturday."

"It's a hard life in the British Police Force," Dylan said.

Sometimes, Clare felt like kicking him. Instead, she followed the sergeant past the closed bar and lounge area, down a corridor to Lecture Theatre One. There was only one double door leading in, which creaked loudly as Ruth opened it.

"You two go in," Chris said, as Ruth closed the door again. "You look like students. Make it discreet. The likelihood is that this guy will turn out to be innocent. We don't want to embarrass him in front of half his friends. I'll cover the door."

The lecture was coming to an end as Clare and Ruth slipped into the room. They looked, but it was hard to identify Swift by the back of his head. As notes were put away and bags closed, the two officers took one side of the room each, checking each face. Clare hoped that the student wasn't skiving off.

He wasn't. She clocked him just as he made his way out of the second row and deliberately brushed against her chest.

"Looking for someone?" he said, with a leering grin.

144

"Craig Swift?"

"You're after me? I'm honoured."

She watched as he appraised her with a chauvinist's eye. Clare decided to forget tact and diplomacy.

"Police," she said. "There are several questions which we would like to ask you. Would you mind accompanying me to the station, please?"

Clare was aware of several people looking around at him. Swift, however, seemed oblivious. As the theatre cleared, Dylan strode down the aisle.

"What's this about?" Swift asked.

"You'll find out," Chris Dylan told him, putting his hand on Swift's shoulder. "Come on, son, don't make any trouble."

Swift looked around and, for a moment, Clare thought he might try and run. Now Ruth joined them, while a gaggle of female students stood in a corner, watching. Craig Swift let them escort him out to the car, and the station.

Three hours later, when he had denied everything, and a search of his bedsit had revealed nothing, they had to let him go.

13

Sophie put the chain across the door before answering it. A big man was blocking the light from the corridor. She was about to slam the door in his face when he spoke.

"Remember me?"

Sophie did. She let him in. "You never told me your name."

"Steve."

"I don't think I thanked you, Steve."

"There was no need to." His voice awkward, anxious. "How are you?"

"Surviving." She motioned him to sit on her plastic chair, but remained standing herself. "Why did you come?"

"To see how you were."

He looked at her with kind eyes. Sophie had begun to use make-up again, to take some care with her appearance. But this guy knew what she was hiding. Nevertheless, she lied.

"I'm fine," she said.

"Have you talked about it with anyone?"

Sophie nodded. Another lie.

"Have you told the police?"

Sophie shook her head. "Have you?" she asked, anxiously.

"No."

A long pause.

"You know," Steve said, "you know he's done it again?"

"I know."

"The thing is … I can't remember if I told you this, but … I saw him."

He was right. Sophie didn't remember.

"It changes things," Steve said.

Tears welled up behind Sophie's eyes. She wanted him to go now. He was another man. He pretended to care, but, really, he wanted to hurt her.

"It changes nothing," Sophie said. "I'm not telling. You have no right to ask me to."

"I wasn't asking you to. But what if…?"

"Go now," Sophie said, raising her voice without meaning to. "Go!"

"I want to help…"

"Go!" She was shouting. She said some other

things, but wasn't sure what words came out, whether they were coherent. Steve was scribbling something on to her notepad.

"My address," he said, softly, "my number. If you…"

Sophie stopped shouting. She was shaking. Steve leant forward. He was going to try and comfort her, like he had tried to last Friday afternoon. But Sophie had no intention of letting him. She wasn't going to let anyone get in close, ever again. She made her body freeze, her muscles tighten. Steve, seeing her reaction, backed off, opened the door.

"Any time you want to call me," he said. "Any time."

He closed the door behind him.

Melanie was in the corridor, on the phone to Lorraine. Lorraine's parents were going to drive her back to Nottingham at the weekend. Melanie arranged to meet her.

"Have you heard anything else from the police?" she asked, as the awkward conversation drew to a halt.

"No," Lorraine said. "They don't know who it was. The more I think about it, the less likely it seems that it would be the guy who tried to pick me up in Rock City. I mean, he'd expect me to recognize him, right?"

"Right."

"And he'd have had to have the ski mask ready in his pocket ... but there was this other guy, who I saw knocking on Sophie's door, a good–looking one..." She described the man she'd seen.

"...the police are looking for him. I don't know, maybe ... all I do know is that I'd be a lot happier coming back to Nottingham if they'd already caught him."

"I understand," Melanie said. "Maybe by Sunday..."

It was a quiet Friday night. Most people were out, but Melanie hadn't felt like socializing. As she put down the phone, she thought she heard a woman shouting. Melanie paused by the phone, trying to work out where it was coming from. The sound stopped. A man was walking down the corridor. The well–built, handsome man with curly brown hair looked at Melanie, saw the fear in her eyes. Then he pushed past her, his face flushed. He was wearing a worn, brown leather flying jacket. He looked exactly like the man who Lorraine had just described to her.

As soon as the man was out of sight, Melanie ran along the corridor, banging on doors.

"Are you all right in there? I heard shouting. Is something wrong?"

She knocked on door after door, repeating the message. No one answered.

Melanie ran down to the foyer. The warden was

off duty. She thought about calling the police, but wasn't sure what to tell them – the man Lorraine had described was in the area, but maybe they had already eliminated him from their inquiries. Maybe she was panicking needlessly. But she had heard a woman's shouts. Suppose she'd been knocked out, or even…?

Melanie ran back up to her room to get Neil's number. There was someone using the phone on her floor. Running back down again, she met a guy on the stairs. He was in his dressing-gown. She recognized him. Chris something. He had asked her out once, but she didn't fancy him, and there was something about his manner which made her wary.

"What's going on?" he asked. "I heard a lot of running about…"

"There was an intruder. I think he's gone now."

"Want me to come downstairs with you?"

"If you wouldn't mind."

Chris accompanied her down into the empty foyer and waited by the booth, looking proprietorial, like he was her boyfriend. Melanie dialled Neil's number. *Please let him be home. Please.* He answered on the second ring. She told Neil what had happened.

"I don't think you're in danger," Neil said. "We know about the guy in the flying jacket. We're looking for him. I'll call it in, straight away. There'll be someone there in—"

"I don't … I don't think I can stay here tonight," Melanie interrupted. "Can I stay with you, please?"

"Of course you can. I'll come and get you."

"I'll be in the foyer."

"Calling the police?" Chris asked.

Melanie nodded. "I think I'll be all right now."

"Are you sure? Do you want me to stay until they come?"

"No. You're shivering. I'll be all right."

"I'm in room B8, if you need me. Good night, Melanie."

"Good night."

Neil arrived two minutes later. Melanie let herself out and got into his car.

"I'm being silly, aren't I?" she said.

"No," he told her. "You're not being silly."

"Only, I spoke to Lorraine today. And the guy she described…"

"I know."

They pulled up outside his small house in Carrington.

"I wish you were coming here under happier circumstances," Neil said.

"So do I."

As Neil made a drink he told her that the police were looking for the guy she'd seen, that he probably wasn't the rapist, but almost certainly was the burglar.

"He used to live in the hall," Neil said. "He's still

got a key. That's how he gets in. But he must be pretty stupid, going back like that." Then Neil sat down beside her on the sofa, leaving a little distance between them.

"Would you hold me, please?" Melanie asked.

For someone so slim, his arms felt surprisingly strong. Melanie had wanted to be with him since that night last week, but she had ruled him out, because he had a girlfriend. Now she saw that the photo on the mantelpiece was gone.

"I know you're only just getting over Clare..." Melanie muttered, guiltily, as they pressed closer together.

"I'm getting over her faster than I thought I would."

Melanie kissed him once, and it was nice. But she wasn't thinking straight, and didn't want to make a mistake. She realized that she was very tired. She realized how afraid she'd been – not just tonight, but for days – and how she had been denying it to herself.

"This isn't the best way to start a relationship, is it?" she said.

"I guess not," Neil replied, disappointment spreading across his face.

"I ought to go to bed."

"You can have mine," he offered. "I'll make one up in the spare room."

"Thanks," she said. "I really appreciate it."

152

Steve didn't know what to do. He had been seen again in Wordsworth Hall. He couldn't go back there. And Sophie wouldn't report the rape. She was disturbed, anyone could see that, but he had no right to tell the police what had happened to her. He should have reported it straight away, but she had begged him not to. And looking after Sophie that afternoon was the only selfless thing he'd done in a long time. How could he betray her?

Sam had advised him to talk to Ruth. Ruth was working on the case, Sam said, and he'd find her easier to talk to than Clare. Steve didn't know. When he was living in the house, he'd never spoken much to Ruth. He found her a bit of a cold fish. And it was her who'd worked out what he was up to. But he had to do something. It felt like what happened to Lorraine Parker was his fault. If the rapist struck again, he would be guilty, too...

Steve walked round to the house. It was only a three minute walk, but he was on edge all the way. It was just after closing time, and there was heavy traffic on the boulevard. Police sirens seemed to stalk the streets. They could be coming after him, Steve thought. And there was still incriminating stuff in his flat. He should lie low. The police didn't know where he lived. But Sam did. She'd promised not to tell. He'd promised to try and persuade Sophie. Now that he'd tried and failed, all bets were off. But the rapist was still out there.

Then the decision was made for him.

"Hey, Steve!"

It was Sam, walking back from the pub with Brian, who lived nearby.

"It's all right," she said to Brian, "Steve can walk me home."

She slipped her arm into his as they turned on to her street.

"Did you see her?"

He told Sam what had happened. Coming to the house, she pointed at the attic.

"There's a light on in Ruth's room."

"The attic?"

"She moved up there last week."

"Isn't it a bit late?"

"She's been working lates. She won't be in bed. Want me to go up first?"

"No. It's all right."

Sam let Steve in.

"Good luck."

Steve walked upstairs. As he walked, he wished that he still lived in the room that he was visiting. He wished that he hadn't let his relationship with Sam slip away. He wished that he'd never stolen anything in his life. But wishes were for children.

There was nothing on TV. Clare was in her nightdress, going through Ruth's books, looking for something to read in bed. Ruth didn't mind her going into her room when she was at work. Since Steve moved out, neither woman kept their door locked. It didn't seem necessary, in an all-woman house. Downstairs, Clare heard the door open and close. It must be Sam, coming in.

Clare had been sleeping badly lately. The case they were working on was getting to her. She had to learn to distance herself, but it wasn't easy. Ruth had several books about women's issues. Maybe that was what Clare needed: a bit of assertiveness training. She looked at the covers: *A Woman in Your Own Right, The Beauty Myth, Backlash*. She was about to pull out one when there was a knock on the door. Sam.

"Come in."

It wasn't Sam. Steve stood in the doorway, wearing the jacket which every witness had identified. Clare began to panic. It was him. He was the rapist. He'd come for her. Or Ruth, it didn't matter. It wasn't Sam she'd heard come in, it was Steve. He must still have his key. She was alone in the house with him. His eyes looked different, scared. His fists were clenched. He was going to hurt her.

"Come any closer and I'll scream," Clare said. "They'll hear me next door."

Steve swore. "I thought you were Ruth," he said. "I wanted..." Then he shook his head, turned round, and went downstairs.

Still shivering, Clare waited until she was sure that he was on the ground floor, then ran down to her room, where she put on her dressing-gown and picked up her truncheon. She wanted to go to the phone, but hadn't heard the front door open or close. Then there was a knock on her door.

"Clare, it's me!"

This time it was Sam. Clare opened it.

"Clare, Steve needs to talk to you. It's important. Please."

Reluctantly, Clare went downstairs.

"What's all this about?"

"It's easier if he explains."

Steve sat in the living-room. Sam put the fire on. Steve spoke, nervously.

"This is off the record, OK?"

"I'm not a journalist," Clare said.

"Please, Clare," Sam pleaded. "This is really important."

"I'm listening," Clare said. "No threats, no promises."

Steve told her his story.

"This second rape," she asked when he'd finished. "Sorry, I meant the first one – of the girl whose name you won't tell me – it happened last Friday?"

"Yes."

"And you've seen her since then?"

"Yes, she went away for a while but she's back now. I saw her today."

"And she won't come forward?"

"No."

Clare knew who it was: Sophie Turner. She had seen the girl yesterday. Now that she knew what had happened, Sophie's behaviour made sense. But there was no point in letting Steve know that she had worked out Sophie's identity.

"And you could definitely identify the bloke?" she asked.

"Definitely."

Clare clapped her hands together and clenched them. At last, they were getting somewhere. She spoke carefully.

"I don't know how we'll deal with the girl who doesn't want to be identified," she said. "But maybe she'll feel different when the guy's behind bars. We've got some photographs – every student at the university. Could you go through them in the morning?"

"Of course."

"Or we might want to take you over to the Clifton Campus, see if you can identify the suspect in the flesh."

"Whatever," Steve assured her.

"I think I'd better ring Neil," Clare said. "See what he says about everything."

She checked her watch. It was nearly midnight. Neil was probably in bed. Never mind. He had a phone at his bedside. For this, he wouldn't mind being woken up. Clare went into the hallway.

The phone rang several times, then was picked up. There was no voice immediately and Clare guessed that she had woken him. It wouldn't be the first time. Neil often got the lead tangled, but he'd never be annoyed, because he knew it would be her. But that was then, and this was...

"Hello?"

A breathy woman's voice.

"Hello?"

Clare cursed silently. She'd got the wrong number and had woken someone else up.

"I'm sorry," she said. "I think I've..."

"Do you want Neil?"

"Eh, yes..."

"Hold on."

A long pause, then:

"Hello?"

Neil's voice this time, gruff, like she was interrupting something. Clare couldn't believe what she was hearing. It was less than a week since she'd split up with him. He was meant to be devastated, not...

"Who is this?" Neil asked, sounding irritated.

"It's Clare," she said, trying to keep her voice calm. "I'm sorry to call at such an inconvenient time, but it's important. Are you awake?"

"I am now."

*   *   *

When he'd finished talking to Clare, Neil put down the phone and turned to Melanie.

"There's a witness," he said. "Someone who's seen the guy we're after."

"Is the rapist the man in the flying jacket?"

"No. Someone else. A student. Look, I have to make another call. Do you want me to use the downstairs phone?"

"No. Stay."

He rang Chris Dylan, waking him, and told the sergeant what Clare had just told him.

"There are a lot of 'ifs' and 'buts'," Dylan said.

"Yes, but the long and short of it is that we can ID the bloke who did it. We should be able to bring him in."

"Yes," Dylan said. "I'll ring the boss. Meet me in the office at eight tomorrow. Bring this Steve Garrett with you."

Neil rang Clare back and arranged to pick Steve up. Then he turned to Melanie.

"I'm afraid I have to get up early in the morning."

He kissed her lightly on the lips, then got up off the bed.

"That woman," Melanie said, "the one who rang. I was sure it was your girlfriend. I thought you were lying about splitting up with her."

"I don't tell lies," Neil said.

"That's nice to hear," Melanie said, affectionately. "It makes you pretty unique."

"Sometimes," Neil said, ruefully, "I'm too nice for my own good."

Reluctantly, before he did something that one of them might regret, he went back up to the spare bedroom.

14

On Saturday morning, the weather was still hot. Kimberley and Cate walked into town together. Kimberley refused to go on the bus, where people could stare at her, say "that's the girl it happened to". Also, the bus went past the house where it happened. It would take Kimberley some time to get used to that.

"Are you coming back to school next week?" Cate asked.

"I don't want to," Kimberley said. "I told Mum I want to change schools, go some place where they don't know about..."

"And what do you do when they find out?" Cate asked. "Change schools again?"

Kimberley was silent. *You can't alter what*

happened. You can't run away from yourself. These were things her mum told her. "You're entitled to still think of yourself as a virgin," Mum said. Maybe she was. But Kimberley had to go to Greencoat for three more years. Wasn't she entitled to privacy, at least? What boy would ask her out when he knew that the first one inside her had been, had been...

Suddenly, out of nowhere, there was a summer storm. Rain pelted down, soaking their thin clothes.

"Let's shelter in the station," Cate suggested.

Kimberley followed her friend into the railway station and they browsed at the bookstall. For once, Kimberley had plenty of money, but she didn't want to waste it on magazines. Her eyes caught that day's edition of the Evening Post. "Slow Progress in Hunt for City Rapist," a small story at the bottom of the front page read. For a horrible moment, she thought that the story might be about her. The police said they'd kept the story out of the papers.

It wasn't. Some man had raped a student in a hall of residence. Kimberley realized why Mum hadn't bought a paper these last two days. *It happens all the time*, Kimberley thought. *It could happen to anyone.* This was what her counsellor kept telling her: *it wasn't your fault*. Kimberley wished that she could believe her.

"It's stopped raining," Cate said. "Shall we go?"

"All right."

"Where shall we go first? HMV?"

The London train had just come in and people swept across the station concourse, some hurrying to be first in the queue for taxis. The girls stopped for a moment rather than be barged aside by impatient travellers. Then one of the people stopped, right in front of her, and smiled.

"Hey, Kim, how you doing?"

She froze.

"Any good parties on tonight?"

Kimberley shook her head, slowly.

"This your friend? What's your name, beautiful?"

Cate looked at Kimberley, unsure what was going on. Kimberley wanted to shout, or scream, or faint ... *something*. Instead, she was frozen to the spot. He looked so ordinary.

"I'm Cate," her friend said.

"Please to meet you, Cate."

He held out his hand and Cate shook it.

"I'm Ashley, but my friends call me Smash."

He smiled. It was a friendly, reassuring smile, which didn't seem to fade, even though he must be able to see the fear in both girls' eyes.

"We must get together sometime, Kim, OK? I've been away for a few days, things to do, y'know. But I'll see you around."

He grinned once more before turning away. Then he walked off, in no particular hurry, a canvas bag casually slung across his shoulder. The two girls stood in the concourse as the station emptied.

"Was that...?" Cate asked.

Kimberley couldn't speak. She was frozen to the spot. She nodded her head.

"There's a phone over there," Cate said, "come on."

But Kimberley couldn't move. Nothing seemed real.

"Come on," Cate repeated. "Oh, look, I'm sorry ... I should have..."

Tears streamed down Kimberley's cheeks and wouldn't stop. She dried them. A moment later, she had to dry them again. She let Cate lead her to the phones, then waited in a daze until one became free.

"What shall I dial?" Cate asked. "999?"

"No. Get my grandfather," Kimberley said. "He'll know what to do." She told her the number and Cate made the call. When it began ringing, she handed the phone to Kimberley. Grandma had to get Grandad out of bed, and it took five ten-pences worth of conversation for Kimberley to stutter out what had happened.

"Stay where you are," Grandad said, when she'd finished. "I'll get someone to come for you."

It took until nine-thirty to get the university administration office open. All the time Chris Dylan spent on the phone, sorting it out, Neil couldn't stop himself thinking about Melanie. He was seeing her again tonight. Neil couldn't believe his luck. He had spent nearly two years pursuing Clare, and ended up with nothing. Then, out of nowhere, Melanie had strayed into his path. What had Clare thought when Melanie answered the phone last night? Neil could guess. Well, let her think it.

"See anyone you recognize?"

Steve shook his head and moved to another page. He was looking at first-year students. The two girls who'd been attacked were first-year students, so there was a fair probability that their attacker was from the same year. When he'd finished going through these thousand odd photos, he'd move on to second-years, then third-years, then post-grads. Steve had also been shown a photograph of Craig Swift, the man who tried to chat Lorraine up at Rock City. It wasn't him.

Neil was worried. It was perfectly possible that the rapist wasn't a student. The rapist could have been on campus for the same reason that Steve was — to commit a crime. The fact that another rape hadn't been reported didn't mean that one hadn't taken place. Two-thirds of rapes weren't reported.

But what would they do if the rapist turned out not to be a student? The police had a description, but a description was rarely enough. They had to find him, and find him quickly. He had raped two women in the space of five days. Unless they found him fast, the chances were that he would strike again, and soon.

Clare wasn't supposed to be on duty. CID had used up their overtime for the week. However, she wanted to know if Steve had identified the rapist yet. She also wanted to know – but didn't expect to find out – who had answered the phone to her last night.

"Any word?" she asked Chris Dylan, who was alone in the Incident Room.

"Not yet. Your friend Steve's been looking at photos for a couple of hours."

"How long did it take Mike Hawkins to pick out Craig Swift?"

"Nearly five hours. Right waste of time."

"It could still be him," Clare argued.

"Not from what your friend Steve says."

"He's not my friend," Clare said.

"He could be making it all up," Dylan suggested. "He could be the one we're after."

"I've thought about it," Clare said. "I don't think he's a rapist."

"All men are potential rapists," Dylan said. "Isn't that what they teach you these days?"

"They teach us to *regard* all men as potential rapists," Clare retorted. "It's not the same thing."

"Explain the difference to me some time, would you?" Dylan said.

"What are we going to do about Steve Garrett's burglaries?" Clare asked.

"It depends," Dylan told her. "Neil put in a lot of time on that case – pity to see it wasted. Why, are you bothered?"

"It puts me in an awkward position," Clare said.

"No," Dylan said. "He put himself in an awkward position. Don't lose any sleep over it."

The phone rang. Clare hoped it would be Neil. But it was Roy Tate. Clare listened to Chris Dylan's end of the conversation.

"She's sure? I see. All right, leave it with me. If you want to. Of course. Top priority. I'll bring in whoever I can." He put down the phone.

"Ashley Smith's back in town. He bumped into Kimberley Pierce just after getting off a train from London."

"She saw him? Did he hurt her?"

Dylan shook his head. "Get this: he asked her whether she knew about any good parties."

Clare swore. Dylan rang the radio operations room, asking them to put officers working the city centre, Meadows and Hyson Green beat on alert for Smith. All officers had already been given Smith's description, but that was five days ago and they would need their memories refreshed. Dylan described the clothes he was wearing today: light blue denim jacket and jeans, white trainers, a red T-shirt.

"If he hasn't gone straight to ground, we should get him," he told Clare.

"But how long will we be able to hold him?" Clare asked.

They looked at each other. Both knew, even before Smith was caught, that the evidence against him would come down to Kimberley's word against his. They needed to get a confession.

"Come on," Dylan said. "Let's go look for him."

They started at the house off Mount Hooton Road which was Ashley Smith's last known address. He must have somewhere to dump his stuff, they figured. If so, this wasn't it. The door, once again, was open, but the house was empty. The bills addressed to Smith were still in the hallway.

"Let's look over the Green," Chris suggested.

Hyson Green had several pubs and two cafés which were regular haunts for drug dealers. If Smash had been in London, the chances were that he was picking up supplies. On return, he would start selling them as quickly as possible, in order to recoup his outlay. But there was no sign of him in any of the obvious places.

"Come on," Dylan said, "it's needle in a haystack time."

They drove to the city centre, parking in Central Police Station. They walked through Trinity Square, across to the Victoria Centre, then down Clumber Street towards the Market Square, looking in likely shops along the way.

Occasionally, when they looked into a record or clothes shop, people gave them odd glances. Clare was dressed like a student, while Chris wore the cheap kind of suit which was usually favoured by male CID officers. They didn't look like a couple. In Yates' Wine Lodge, Clare was spotted by Max, a boy she'd gone out with when she was at sixth form college. She hadn't seen him in two years, so he didn't know that she was in the force. Max gave Chris a peculiar look, then frowned at Clare. What was she doing with this straight-looking guy, ten years older than her?

Two hours had passed since Roy Tate rang in to report Smash's return to Nottingham. It was unlikely that he was still in the city centre. They finished their search in Hockley, looking in the gyms and a snooker club which he might belong to. There was no sign of him. Nor was there any sign of Roy Tate, who'd said that he would catch them up in the city centre. Nottingham was not a huge city, but it was big enough to miss someone in.

"What now?" Clare asked.

"The Meadows?"

"You're kidding – this afternoon?"

It was the last full day of the football season and Forest, the local Premier League side, were playing at home. Supporters were streaming through the city in a last minute rush to get to the game, many of them walking through the Meadows area and the Maynard Estate. The officers on duty at the game would have Smash's description, but he could easily hide in the crowd.

"I think we're stuck," Chris said. "I'm going to ring Neil, see if he's got anywhere."

Clare knew Neil would have paged them if Steve had identified the rapist, but said nothing. She waited while Chris made the call. The afternoon was becoming frustrating. But frustration was the story of her life. If you didn't have the patience to play a waiting game, you weren't cut out for CID.

Chris came out of the phone box.

"He's gone through nearly all the photos. No luck."

"So our man isn't a student."

"Or the file photo's a bad likeness. Or the guy's changed in appearance since the photo was taken. The photos they use are little passport ones, taken when they apply for a place. People can change between seventeen and twenty."

"True."

Clare remembered herself at seventeen. She'd been so happy-go-lucky, dating a string of boys, unable to decide whether to do architecture at university or something sexier, like film studies, or photography. When had she last picked up a camera? When had she last gone out dancing? A gruff voice interrupted her thoughts.

"Any joy?"

Out of uniform, Roy Tate looked his age — a balding man with flushed cheeks and bags beneath his eyes. He was sweating profusely beneath his heavy, old-fashioned grey sports jacket. Roy was too old to be chasing round the city like he was John Wayne in *The Searchers*.

"I'm sorry," Dylan said. "Nothing. I think we're going to head back to the office for now. Can we give you a lift?"

Roy shook his head. "I'm going to walk round a bit more, then go to my daughter's, see how Kimberley is. You can call me there if anything comes up."

"Fine," Dylan said. "I hope she's all right. It must have been a big shock for the kid, seeing him again that way."

"Not as big a shock as he's going to get when he runs into me."

Chris put an arm on Roy's shoulder. "Don't do anything daft, Roy. We'll get him."

"He's got off twice," Roy reminded them.

"Third time lucky," Chris said.

But he didn't sound convinced.

Clare and Chris walked back to the central police station in silence, scarcely bothering to look in the shops this time. Smash Smith had gone to ground. Half the criminals in Nottingham knew that they were looking for him, so Smash, too, would know by now. If he stayed in a safe house, there was nothing they could do. In a way, Clare thought, Smith was in prison. But that thought wouldn't comfort Roy Tate, or his granddaughter.

"You're not being paid for this, you know," Chris said, as they walked into the car park.

"Neither are you."

"Yeah, but CID's my job. You're only an aide. I'll run you home on my way to the office if you like."

Clare shook her head. "I want to see this through to the conclusion."

"I doubt that anything else is going to happen this afternoon," Chris told her. "We'll give it another hour, then call it a day. Let's go back to the office."

They were getting into the car when a uniformed PC came running out of the station into the car park.

"Excuse me, sir, but there's a bloke waiting for you. We've been trying to page you since two, but your battery must be flat."

Chris cursed. "All right. We're coming."

He and Clare walked into the station.

"They know I'm not officially on duty today," Chris said. "So, whoever it is, they should have told him to go away. I've got better things to do than…"

"Chris," Clare said, quietly. "Look."

There, sitting in the waiting area, was a young man of twenty or so, with a light blue denim jacket and jeans, a red T-shirt and white trainers. He stood up.

"My friends tell me that you're looking for me," the young man said. "I thought I'd come in, save you some trouble."

Neil and Clare were speechless.

"Now," said Ashley Smith, "what seems to be the problem?"

15

In Wordsworth Hall, Melanie helped Lorraine sort out her new room. Someone had dropped out earlier in the year and the Warden suggested that she might like a move. A porter was permanently on duty in the foyer now and the new room had been fitted with a triple lock. The university had also put up a notice promising that, over the summer, they would put equally strong locks on all the rooms, and install a video surveillance system. Better late than never, Melanie said, but Lorraine had no intention of coming back to Wordsworth Hall next term.

"Do you want to talk about it?" Melanie asked, when they stopped for coffee.

Lorraine shook her head. "I've hardly talked

about anything else since Wednesday night. Tell me what you've been doing."

Melanie hesitated. Lorraine guessed why.

"You've started seeing someone?"

She smiled and made her eyes go goofy for a moment. That meant it was serious.

"What's his name?"

"Neil."

"What's he study?"

"He doesn't. He's in the police. He's the bloke I told you about – the one who gave me a lift to the party, Friday before last."

"I thought you said he had a girlfriend?"

"He did. They split up the next day."

"Good timing," Lorraine said.

"According to him, it was her idea – the whole relationship was a bit of a disaster, but he asked her to … never mind. Anyway, I saw him again on Thursday. Then on Friday, I got into a real tizz because I thought I'd seen the guy who attacked you and I was scared, so I asked if I could go to his house and…"

"And one thing led to another?"

"Not yet. But I'm seeing him again tonight."

Lorraine smiled. She didn't want Melanie to feel guilty about getting some joy out of her misfortune. She was only relieved to be talking about something positive. As Melanie started to describe Neil, Lorraine realized that he was the same bloke who'd been to see her about the burglary – a wiry, fair-haired, local type. Not bad looking, but nothing special, to her eyes. That was Melanie for you: she was always being chased by good-looking men, but preferred mild, younger brother types.

"He's sweet," Melanie was saying, "and shy. You know, it's really liberating – I'm the one making all the moves."

"How old is he?"

"Twenty-two, three, something like that. He seems younger. Not that experienced. I think his last girlfriend treated him like a floorcloth."

They finished their coffee and went back to work. Melanie held up a Salvador Dalí poster.

"Where do you want to put this?"

Lorraine's good mood evaporated. She took the poster from Melanie without speaking. Then she closed her eyes, trying to hold off a flashback of herself focusing on the poster when the masked man was raping her. She'd stared at the surreal images, trying to disassociate herself from what was happening, failing.

"I don't," she said.

"Pardon? What's wrong?"

Instead of replying, Lorraine started swearing, screwing the poster up in her hands until it was a tight, compacted ball.

"I'm sorry," Lorraine said, as she threw the ball in the bin.

"No. I'm sorry."

As the two women hugged, there was a knock on the door. Melanie broke away and opened it.

"Oh. Hi."

It was Sophie from down the corridor. She looked pale and guilty. Sophie had been meant to go to the concert with Lorraine, but had disappeared for days, without explanation.

"Come in," Lorraine told her.

Lorraine tried to get everything back into focus. She knew that Sophie probably blamed herself in some way for what had happened. Sophie would figure that, if she'd been there, Lorraine would not have walked home alone. Lorraine had been over every if-I-hadn't-done-this and if-only-I'd-done-that in her mind. But what happened happened. She didn't want to talk about the rape, yet she didn't want Sophie to feel in the least responsible, either.

"Can I talk to you," Sophie asked, "alone?"

Melanie looked at Lorraine.

"Thanks for helping," Lorraine said.

"I'm meant to be seeing Neil tonight," Melanie told her, "but not till late. If you want, I can put him off. Or you could come out for a drink with us?"

"I'll see how it goes," Lorraine said.

"I'll look in later."

Then Lorraine was alone in the room with Sophie.

"You look worse than I feel," she told her friend.

"You don't know the half of it," Sophie said, then sat down on the edge of the bed.

"What is it?" Lorraine asked.

Sophie began to cry.

"Come on," Lorraine said.

It made a change to be comforting someone, rather than be comforted. She put an arm round her friend.

"What is it?"

"It's all my fault," Sophie said.

"Don't be daft," Lorraine told her. "You weren't to know, when you went away..."

"But I was," Sophie said. "You see, it happened to me, too."

At first, Clare thought it must be a case of mistaken identity. Even the most stupid criminal didn't walk into a police station, giving himself up, then decline legal representation – not if he had something to hide. Ashley Smith sat in the pale green interview room, leaning back confidently as the tape recorder was switched on.

"What's all this about, then?" he asked.

Chris Dylan was doing the interview. Clare was watching from outside the room.

"Where were you last Saturday night, Ashley?"

He thought for a moment.

"Early evening, in the Feathers. There must be ten, a dozen people saw me there. About ten, I went to a party. Don't know the address. A squat on the edge of the Maynard Estate."

"What happened at the party?"

Smith smiled. "I had a few drinks, a few smokes, a bit of a dance…"

"And…?"

Smith's eyes narrowed. Then he smiled. "And a bit of the other. Is that what this is about?"

"You tell me."

The smile remained fixed on Smith's face.

"I don't want to walk into anything."

"Did you do anything wrong?" Dylan asked.

"Wrong? Me? No way."

"Well, then. Why don't you tell me about it? Clear things up?"

"Like what?"

"Let's take it slowly." Dylan's voice was calm, re-assuring. "Did you meet a girl at this party?"

"Yes."

"How did you meet her?"

"She was with some bloke. A Paki. He wasn't treating her right. I got involved."

"You hit him?"

"Is he the one complaining? Is that what this is about?"

Dylan didn't reply. He repeated the question.

"You hit him?"

"I gave him a little smack, yeah."

"What happened next?"

"He got out of the way."

"And the girl?"

"She was ... you know ... grateful."

"Describe her to me."

Smith bobbed his head up and down a little, as
though the effort of recollection required physical
movement.

"Long brown hair, about five-one or two, tight
dress, nice figure."

"What was her name?"

"Kim."

"How old would you say she was?"

"Seventeen, eighteen. Is that what this is about?"

"What?"

"Her age. Thing is, I bumped into her again
today, this morning – you know, in daylight. And I
wanted to see her again, but she looked a bit young,
you know. I thought, without make-up, she might
only be fifteen, sixteen."

At this point, Clare would have been tempted to
tell him how old Kimberley really was, but Dylan
didn't. It made no difference anyway. Smash was
under twenty-four, and, therefore, according to
official guidelines, wouldn't be prosecuted for
unlawful sexual intercourse. The law let him off if
he had good reason to believe the girl was over
sixteen – something which was practically
impossible to prove either way. Clare thought that
this was wrong, but it was the law.

"Tell me what happened," Dylan continued, "from the moment you met her."

Smith shrugged. "I don't remember precisely. We clicked, you know. We talked for a bit, then she asked if there was anywhere we could go."

"*She* asked?"

"Yeah. So I thought, *I'm in here*, and took her upstairs. The bedrooms were in use, so we used the bathroom. You can imagine the rest."

Clare watched Dylan's face. He smiled at Smith, as though the two of them were men together, chatting over a drink in a pub. He didn't mean it. He was doing what they trained you to do, building a rapport with the criminal. Clare wasn't sure if she could ever pretend the way Chris was doing. It was hard enough sitting outside the room, listening to a rapist boast about what he'd done to a thirteen-year-old girl.

"You had sex?" Dylan asked, softly.

"Yeah."

"Describe it to me."

"Aw, come on."

"You took her upstairs to the bathroom. You locked the door."

"I don't think the door locked. Maybe it did. I don't remember. I don't think Kim was worried about privacy, know what I mean?"

"No. I don't know. Tell me."

"You want me to spell it out?" Smith said, with

an arrogant swagger to his voice.

"Yes."

"She was begging for it."

Dylan was silent for a moment. When he spoke again, his voice was softer, more friendly.

"And you gave it to her?"

"Yeah."

"All right, Ashley, do me a favour here. Give me the details."

Clare knew what Dylan was trying to do. In describing a sequence of events which didn't take place – Kimberley consenting to sex – Smith was likely to make mistakes. Dylan would give him as much rope as possible to hang himself with, then tighten the noose, pointing out the contradictions in his story. Smith might not confess, but a jury reading the transcript would know that he'd been lying, even if he had the story fully sorted out by the time he got to court.

Dylan summed up the story so far. "You got into the bathroom. You shut the door. Maybe you locked it. What happened then?"

Smith sneered. "You're a dirty old man, aren't you? This is how you get your kicks, innit? Hearing me tell how I had it away with a young girl. You haven't got the balls to do it yourself, but you like to hear about it."

Dylan didn't rise to the bait. He tried again.

"All right. She was young. She was in a tight

dress. She was begging for it. You gave it to her."

"If you want to put it that way."

"Did you ask her, first?"

"How do you mean?"

Dylan smiled, man to man. "She might have been teasing you, leading you on. How did you know that she wanted to go the whole way?"

Smith laughed. Clare wondered if he realized how vital his next answer was. The issue of consent was crucial.

"Look," he said, still laughing. "We get into the room. She gets a condom out of her bag. I didn't have to ask."

This threw Dylan. "You wore a condom," he said, disbelievingly.

"Course I did. You never know where the little slag's been, do you?"

"Describe the sequence," Dylan said, slowly. "You're saying that you went into the bathroom, she handed you a condom, you undressed, then put it on. Yes?"

"No. She put it on. Not straight away. First, she…"

Clare couldn't listen any longer. Smith was making up filth about Kimberley Pierce, filth which he would repeat in court, if it got to court, to be listened to by Kimberley's parents and grand-parents. This afternoon, Dylan would have to listen to it, pretend to believe it, then go over it all again, and again, until Smith started making mistakes, or the detective sergeant gave up.

Clare went to the office and waited. Fifteen minutes later, Dylan joined her.

"Having a break?" she asked, getting up to make him a coffee.

Chris shook his head. "I started pressing him too hard and he asked for a lawyer. How much did you hear?"

"Enough. What now?"

Dylan sighed and sat down. "We keep him for twenty-four hours. We search the address he's given us, though God knows what we can expect to find there. He'll have cleaned the place out before coming in. We pass the paperwork to the CPS. Then we let him go."

The Crown Prosecution Service, Clare knew, would only prosecute if there was more than a fifty per cent chance of conviction. The CPS only took one in five rape cases to court. The chances in this case were practically zero.

"The thing is," Chris said, "he's been through the ropes before. He's been in court for rape and attempted rape. God knows how many others he's got away with. And he's going to keep doing it."

Dylan took a sip of coffee, then picked up the phone. "Better talk to the boss."

He was on the phone for less than two minutes.

"Well?" Clare asked, when he was done.

"We should have the warrant in half an hour. Then we go over to his place, see if we turn anything up."

"And if we don't?"

"Then we let him go."

Sophie and Lorraine sat on Lorraine's bed. Sophie had described what happened to her eight days before. Now she was trying to explain why she hadn't told anyone.

"It happened to a friend of mine," Sophie explained, "two years ago. Louise went out with this guy once and dropped him. A month later, he talked her into going back to his house, beat her up and raped her. When it went to court, she felt like she was the one on trial. The defence made her feel like a prostitute. They convinced the jury that they were already lovers, that it was rough sex, that it got out of hand, that it was Louise's fault. He got off.

"When it happened to me ... I'm sorry, Lorraine – I know if I'd gone to the police, he might not have ... but I couldn't, I couldn't face going through what Louise had to go through. She said the trial and everything that went with it was far worse than the rape itself."

"I understand," Lorraine said, "really, I do. But if this bloke, Steve, saw the guy who attacked you, then surely..."

"It doesn't matter," Sophie said. "Unless they

catch the guy when they're actually attacking you, he'll get off. They always do."

"That's not what the police say," Lorraine told her. "They say that, most of the time, when it's a stranger, they're found guilty. You didn't know the guy, did you? He was wearing a mask, wasn't he?"

"Yes," Sophie said. "So how will they ever prove who he is?"

Lorraine said nothing. She could understand Sophie not wanting people to know – Lorraine felt the same way. She didn't blame Sophie. But she didn't know how to help her, either.

"Did you tell your parents what happened?" she asked.

Sophie shook her head. "I haven't talked to anyone, until today. You don't know my parents. I couldn't upset them that way, not after what happened to Louise."

"What about your friend Louise?" Lorraine asked. "Couldn't you call her?"

"No, I couldn't," Sophie said. "You see, Louise left town. Everyone knew what had happened to her. She couldn't deal with that. So she just left, started again somewhere else. I haven't heard from her since. Before this happened, I couldn't understand how she could do that. But now I can. Can you?"

"Yes," Lorraine said. "Yes, I can."

16

"Is that all of them?" Steve asked.

"That's all of them," Neil told him.

"What now?" Steve asked.

Neil thought about it. Steve was fed up. Neil didn't blame him, but at least Steve had something to do. Neil had spent the last few hours watching Steve flick through photograph after photograph. As well as the student photos, he'd looked at shots of known sexual offenders, not matching any of them. The afternoon was nearly over. Neil had failed to get a result.

"What do we do now?" Steve repeated.

What was Neil doing here, wasting his afternoon with a known thief, who, Neil half guessed, was only helping because he knew the police had him thoroughly stitched up for a string of petty burglaries? Neil found Steve arrogant and irritating, not to mention pathetic – doing what he did after all those years of education. But he wasn't going to let him off the hook. The rapist was probably there, but the photo was a bad likeness. Neil sighed, picked up the first pile of application forms, each holding a passport-sized photo of the student at seventeen, and handed them to Steve.

"We start all over again," he said.

By six in the evening, Sophie had almost made up her mind to go to the police, tell them what had happened. She and Lorraine walked round to Steve Garrett's flat together. There was no one in. Sophie left him a note.

"I need to talk," it read. "Please come and see me this weekend, Sophie."

"Do you think he'll come?" Lorraine asked, as they walked back to hall.

"I think so. He seems like a nice guy."

"What does he look like?"

Sophie described him. Lorraine groaned.

"Of course, he's the guy I saw knocking on your door. I told the police about him."

"You what?"

Lorraine nodded. "And I told Melanie, too. Her new boyfriend checked him out."

"And?"

"And he told her that he almost certainly wasn't the rapist, but he was the burglar."

This time, Sophie groaned. "So, if I tell the police about him, I get him into trouble."

"You lose your privacy. He loses his liberty."

"What am I going to do?"

Sophie let them back into the hall with the new key which the university had provided the day before. The porter who was permanently on duty in the hall made sure that any visitors signed themselves in. An intruder would have trouble getting by unseen. In the foyer, Chris Williams, who had asked Sophie out a couple of times, said hello to both of them. He smiled sympathetically at Lorraine, then spoke to Sophie.

"I haven't seen you around for a while. Have you been ill?"

"Family things to sort out."

That was the line she'd decided to take about why she went away. No one wanted to ask questions about family problems: death, divorce, illness. You came to university and your friends became your family – if you were lucky. Sophie had never been too great at making and keeping friends.

"Going out tonight?" Chris asked. "There's a few of us going for a drink at…"

"Actually," Sophie said, "Lorraine and I are meeting some friends for a meal."

"Oh. Fine. Have a nice night."

"You too, Chris."

"So," Lorraine said, when they were climbing the stairs, "we're meeting some friends, are we?"

"Oh, you know me. I didn't want to hurt his feelings. Anyway, I thought we might go and see our friends at Pancho's Fish Bar, get a take-out."

"Sounds fine to me," Lorraine said. "But I don't think I'll be hungry for a while."

"No. Me neither. Let's wait and see if Steve shows up."

"I dunno," Lorraine said. "Do you think he'll want to show his face round here again?"

Before Sophie could reply, a Birmingham accent interrupted them.

"Hey, Lorraine."

It was Mark Brewer, from the floor above. Sophie only knew him to nod to, but thought he was a bit of a creep. Lorraine greeted him politely.

"Hi, Mark."

"Have you heard anything from the police about those burglaries yet?"

"Sorry, no. I've put in an insurance claim. What about you?"

Brewer shrugged. "I have to pay the first twenty-five pounds on the credit card bill because I didn't report it straight away. But it's not that I mind – it's the fact that someone's done that to me – you know?"

Sophie couldn't believe it. Everyone in the hall

must know by now that Lorraine had been raped on Wednesday night, yet here was Mark asking for sympathy because someone had nicked his credit card.

The phone on their corridor began to ring.

"Excuse me," Sophie said.

Mark continued to talk to Lorraine as Sophie answered the phone.

"Do you think you could get Melanie in C3 for me, please? This is Neil."

"I'll see if she's in."

Melanie came to the phone. Sophie heard her speaking to her boyfriend.

"Have you got anywhere? No. I'll stay in and wash my hair. Don't worry. It'd be nice if you could make it for a last drink. All right, I'll expect you then."

As Mark Brewer walked down the stairs, Lorraine asked Melanie if there was any news.

"I don't know. He doesn't really tell me … they're questioning someone, that's why he's going to be late."

"A suspect?" Sophie asked, her heart beginning to race.

"No. A possible witness. Do you two want to get some food later?"

The three of them agreed to go for a take-out at around nine. Sophie and Lorraine went back to Sophie's room together. Neither of them wanted to be alone.

*　　*　　*

Roy Tate put down the telephone.

"What is it?" his daughter asked.

Kimberley sat in front of the TV set with the sound down low. It was four hours since they'd heard that the man who'd attacked her had given himself up. Kimberley was better at waiting than Roy was. She seemed to have turned herself back into a little girl. She'd even started sucking her thumb again, something she stopped doing long before secondary school. It broke his heart to look at her that way.

"Dad?" Karen said, coming over to him. "Dad, why are you crying?"

Roy didn't answer. He'd known that this was the way it was likely to go, but he hadn't admitted it to himself, hadn't worked out what he was going to do. It was a head versus heart thing: in his head, he was as cynical as the next copper; in his heart, he had this stupid idea that justice would prevail.

"Grandad," Kimberley asked. "Grandad, what's happened?"

She had, he saw, turned off the TV. The room was silent, except for the sound of his breathing, which was absurdly loud. His wife came over and handed him a handkerchief. The three women who made up his life all stood around him now, waiting for him to speak. He ought to be able to reward their love by protecting them. He ought to be able to...

"Roy," his wife, Joyce, said, in a stern voice, "come on."

He pulled himself together.

"They let the bastard go," he told them. "They said they could have held him longer, but there was no chance of it holding up in court, so they've let the bastard go."

Karen put an arm around Kimberley, who looked numb. Joyce, too, embraced her granddaughter. Roy stood up and put his coat on.

"Roy," Joyce said. "Roy, where are you going?"

"Ring in sick for me," he told her as he walked to the door.

"Dad," Karen called, "what are you going to do?"

"I don't know," Roy said. "I really don't know."

"I'll give you a ride home," Chris told Clare, as they left the CID office.

"It's all right," she told him. "I can walk."

"You've done enough walking, and you're on my way. Hold on while I make a call."

Clare couldn't help overhearing Dylan talking to his wife, apologizing for not taking the kids somewhere or other. His voice on the phone was gentle, almost whining, in strong contrast to his professional manner. Then it became terser.

"No, I can't. There's something else going on. If it comes up ... I know what I said. Look, I'll pay for a sitter, all right? All right!"

193

He slammed the phone down and sighed. Then he rang Neil.

"How's it going? OK. Give it another hour. I don't care if he's getting bored. If he threatens to leave, charge him with burglary, that should shut him up."

"Are you really going to charge Steve?" Clare asked, as they got into Chris's car.

"That depends on whether his information leads to a conviction," Chris told her. "If it doesn't, then at least we've cleared up half a dozen burglaries. You didn't make him any promises, did you?"

"Not as such," Clare told him.

"Never make promises you can't keep. They always backfire on you. Like me taking the kids to Wollaton Park this afternoon."

"There'll be other days," Clare said, trying to be friendly.

"Not if my ex-wife has her way and moves to Devon with her new boyfriend."

"Oh."

Clare hadn't realized that Dylan was divorced. He didn't wear a ring, but neither did a lot of married men in the force.

"Too many broken promises," Dylan said, "that's why she divorced me. I'm meant to have the kids tonight, but suppose Neil comes up with a name? We can't leave it until Monday – he might strike again. So I have to carry a bleeper, which means I can't look after the kids on my own, which means that Jenny has to get a babysitter so she and her boyfriend can go out to dinner."

"Someone else could cover it," Clare suggested. "Neil…"

"Neil's meant to be seeing his girlfriend tonight."

Clare winced as he pulled up outside her house.

"I've got my pager," she told him. "If anything does come up, I'd like you to call me, please."

"All right," Dylan said. "I'll call you."

He looked at his watch. It was just after seven.

"Time to go and eat some humble pie," he said.

Clare walked into the house to the smell of Sam's home-made pizza. Her landlady and Ruth were sitting at the kitchen table, eating together.

"Is there enough of that for me to have some?" she asked.

"Sure," Sam said, "we can open some wine if you like. I fancied some, but Ruth isn't drinking."

"Not for me," Clare told her. "I'm kind of on duty, too."

"Why?" Ruth asked.

Clare and Sam exchanged glances. Ruth didn't know about Steve and the burglaries. Now didn't feel like the time to tell her.

"It's complicated," she said. "I'm afraid I have some bad news about Roy's granddaughter."

When Clare finished talking, Ruth shook her head despairingly.

"What can you do?" she said.

"I don't know," Clare told her. "If the girl had reported it straight away, we'd almost certainly have him…"

"Would we?" Ruth said. "Nothing's certain in cases like that. And why should we expect her to behave that way? Put yourself in the place of a thirteen-year-old girl who that's happened to – how would you feel? Scared, confused, ashamed. What's the most natural thing to do in that situation? Pretend it didn't happen."

"I guess you're right," Clare said, "but if people behave that way, how are we ever going to convict—"

"We're not," Ruth interrupted. "Men get away with it, all the time, unless they're incredibly stupid or unlucky. You can't rely on the law where anything to do with sex is concerned."

Clare and Sam were silent. Sometimes, Ruth went off on anti-men rants like this, and it was best to let her get it out of her system. But Ruth, it turned out, had finished talking. Clare helped herself to more salad to go with her pizza.

"What are you doing tonight?" Sam asked her.

"If my pager doesn't go, I thought you and I might rent a video," Clare said.

"I am honoured," Sam told her. "I thought, now that you're single again, men would be breaking down the doors trying to get to you."

"The news obviously hasn't spread yet," Clare

said. "Mind you, Neil's got someone."

"You're kidding?" Ruth jumped in. "Already?"

Clare nodded. "I had to ring him late on Thursday night – a woman answered the phone. Then Chris Dylan told me he'd promised Neil he could get off later so that he could meet his girlfriend."

"How many single women are there in CID?" Ruth asked.

"There's only Tracey in his team," Clare told her, "and it wasn't her voice."

"Are you jealous?" Sam asked.

Clare thought about her reply. "I'll have to let you know when I see him with her. I guess I'm kind of … disappointed that he could start with someone else so quickly. I mean … he was supposed to be so serious about me. He wanted to…"

"Don't be so precious," Sam said. "It's like riding a bike. He fell off, so he's got on again as quickly as possible. I'll bet he has a string of girlfriends over the next few months. He has something to prove to himself, and something to prove to you."

"Neil's not like that," Clare said.

"Then he's one of the few," Ruth told her.

"What I ought to do," Sam said, "is to take you to a club tonight. We could both do with some male company."

"Another time," Clare said.

You never met decent men in clubs, not in her

experience. But if not there, where? The last thing Clare wanted was a relationship with another policeman. Chris Dylan wasn't unusual. The job had more divorces than practically any other career. And Clare was choosy. At university, she had been chased by men all the time, but she had only met one who she thought she could fall in love with. In the months when she wasn't going out with Neil, she had only had one date, with a doctor. He was nice, but, finally, too old and boring for her. Maybe she'd made a mistake splitting up with Neil. Why did he have to ask her to marry him?

"It isn't nine yet," Sam told Ruth as she left the table.

"I want to get in early, talk to Roy."

"What's the news on Steve?" Sam asked, when Ruth was gone.

"Nothing. He's gone through all the photos twice. He's still doing it now, as far as I know. Neil's with him."

"And if they don't find the rapist, what about the burglaries?"

"That's not up to me," Clare said. "It's up to Neil."

Outside, it was turning dark. The CID clock showed ten past nine.

"All right," Neil told Steve. "That's the lot."

"I'm really sorry," Steve said. "You know, he

198

might be in there, but, if he is, his photo doesn't look like he does. What do we do now?"

"We do nothing until Monday. Then we take you to the Clifton campus and you hang around, trying to spot this guy."

"Fine."

"I'll run you home," Neil said. "Let me make a call first."

He rang the number for the phone on Melanie's corridor. No one answered. She was probably washing her hair, Neil thought, not expecting him to be through yet. He would drop off Steve, go home, get changed, then take her out for a drink at the time they'd agreed, ten. He could hardly wait.

17

"Let's go in the Grosvenor," Lorraine suggested, as they passed the busy pub on their way back from a fish and chip supper. "It's too early to go home."

"I'm meeting Neil," Melanie said, "but we could join you later."

Sophie looked dubious. Melanie didn't know why she seemed so depressed. Anyone would think that she was the one who'd been raped, not Lorraine.

"Come on," Lorraine said to her. "I'm buying."

Sheepishly, Sophie followed Lorraine into the pub.

Melanie walked back to hall alone, thinking about Lorraine, and how she was getting by. She was the sort of person, Melanie thought, who could cope with what had happened to her. She would get over it because she had to.

Or would she? Melanie didn't really know how Lorraine was taking it. Did anyone ever really know themselves, never mind anybody else? Melanie couldn't tell how she'd cope if it happened to her. The whole thing made her angry, like she wasn't in complete control of her life. Even now, making a short, twilight walk, she felt afraid, and wished Neil was with her. She resented herself relying on a man, no matter how nice he was.

Melanie walked past Clarendon College and crossed Sherwood Rise. A black guy in a big car slowed down and gave her a good looking over. Melanie walked faster, wishing that she wasn't wearing a dress, wishing that she was invisible, wishing she'd gone to the pub with Sophie and Lorraine. She sighed with relief as she opened the door to Wordsworth Hall and crossed the foyer. She felt sticky from the evening heat. There wasn't time to wash her hair, but maybe she could take a shower.

"I'm expecting someone called Neil Foster," she told the night porter. "The policeman. I'm telling you now in case I'm in the shower when he arrives. Could you let him go straight upstairs after he's signed in?"

"All right, duck," said the porter, with a wink.

Melanie hurried up the stairs. What did the

porter think she was getting at? Oh, let him think what he wanted.

Melanie checked that the bathroom nearest her room was free, then went into her room and undressed. Until this week, she'd always left her door open when she went for a shower. Now she locked it and took the key in her sponge bag, even though it was inconvenient. Neil could wait in the corridor if necessary. Melanie locked the bathroom door behind her, switched the shower on, and waited for the water to heat up.

Steve got home at half past nine, tired and hungry. Passport photo faces floated in front of his eyes. He felt annoyed with himself: what if one of them had been the rapist? He tried to picture the man now, but the image resolutely failed to flicker into view.

In his dingy hallway, Steve almost missed the note. The scrap of paper looked like it had fallen from one of the free newspapers which littered the hall. Sophie hadn't put a time on it, but it must have come today. What did it mean? Maybe she'd decided to go to the police after all.

In his small kitchen, Steve realized that he'd forgotten to buy food. There was a store up the road which was open until ten-thirty, or he could get a take-away. Should he go and see Sophie? His head ached and he didn't want to deal with her now. Even so, something compelled him to see what she wanted. The likelihood was that she wouldn't be in. He would leave a note and his conscience would be satisfied.

Steve set out into the darkening evening and made the short walk to Wordsworth Hall. He was about to use his key to get in when he spotted a porter behind the counter, looking in his direction. They had obviously upped the security. He pressed the buzzer instead.

The lock had been changed, Steve realized, as the middle-aged man let him in. His key wouldn't have worked anyhow. If he'd used it, he would have given himself away.

"Yes?"

"I'm here to see Sophie Turner, C floor."

"If you'll wait a moment, I'll see if she's in."

The porter picked up the phone and rang the floor. After half a minute, he shook his head.

"Sorry, no one in on that floor."

"All right," Steve said. "I'll leave her a note."

The porter lent him a pen and paper. Steve tried to think of what to say. In the end, he settled for, "I called. You were out. Will try again. Steve."

Just as he was handing the note in, someone came by and checked the pigeon-holes. Most of them had a flyer for a taxi firm in them. The room's occupants had gone out, but not yet come back in. Steve saw the guy in profile and froze. A large hand reached out to one of the compartments, even though it was obviously empty. He must have picked up his flyer earlier. Steve turned away quickly, in case, this time, the guy recognized him.

"Good night, sir," the porter said, prompting Steve to leave.

As he was shown to the door, Steve risked a glance back, just in time to see the rapist walking back up the staircase, emptyhanded. Why was he checking the pigeon-holes? Luckily, all the rooms on C floor appeared to be empty. But supposing someone came back?

While he was thinking about this, the porter, who seemed to find Steve suspicious, opened the door for him. Should Steve say something? But it was too late, the door was shutting behind him. Steve stepped out into the night and began to run.

"Where's Roy?" Ruth asked, as she arrived.

"Called in sick."

Ruth knew the reason why.

"What am I on tonight?" she asked her sergeant.

"In a car with Brian, when he shows up. Nasreen's got paperwork to do."

As Ruth made coffee, the afternoon shift started to roll in. If criminals were intelligent, these were the periods when they would commit crimes: at six, two and ten, when the shifts changed over and response times were way down.

"Did you hear about Ashley Smith?" Ruth overheard someone asking. Smith's photo was pinned to the noticeboard. Everyone now knew what had happened to Roy's granddaughter.

"If he so much as drops a piece of litter in this city," another commented, "he'll find himself behind bars before he knows what's hit him."

It was macho, meaningless talk. In the old days, someone would have fitted Smash Smith up for something other than rape, and the courts would have gone along with it. Today, the courts were less reliable and an officer caught fabricating evidence would be dismissed. They would lose their pension, and might end up in prison themselves. It wasn't worth it, not even for the sake of putting away an evil sod like Smith.

"Looks like you and me, then," Brian said, sitting down next to Ruth.

She nodded.

"This was the last straw for Roy," Brian told her. "He'll be putting in for his pension now."

"Do you really think so?" Ruth asked.

Roy had already put in his thirty years. He always said he liked the job too much to leave.

"I don't think so, I know so," Brian insisted. "Word is, he came in earlier today and cleared out his locker."

"Oh."

Ruth felt sad and a little betrayed. Roy was her mentor. She would have liked to hear it from him.

But he didn't owe her anything. She couldn't blame him for wanting to get out.

She checked the noticeboard. There were two bail absconders, three stolen cars and a flasher hanging around Mapperley Park. Also on the board was the address the police had for Ashley Smith, a flat above a shop on the edge of Ruth's beat, in Sherwood. If Smith had any sense, he would get out of Nottingham quickly. It would be impossible for him to carry on his previous occupation, drug dealing. Even if he went straight, joined a church, devoted his life to charitable activity, he would be continually harassed by every officer he came across, until he got put away or left for good.

It was five to ten.

"Shall we be getting out?" Ruth asked Brian.

"Let me finish this coffee first. There's no hurry. We might not get another break all night."

Ruth made a mental note of Ashley Smith's address, hoping against hope that she got some excuse to nick him.

Clare and Sam slumped on the sofa, watching a video of *What's Eating Gilbert Grape?* Someone started banging loudly on the front door. Sam pressed the pause button on the remote control. Clare followed her into the hallway.

"Who is it?" Sam asked, starting to put the chain across the door.

"Steve." His voice sounded urgent. "Is Clare there?"

"What's going on?" Clare asked, as Sam let him in.

"I saw him, at the hall, five minutes ago. He lives there. In Room B8, I think."

"The rapist?"

"Yes."

"Have you called it in?"

"There isn't a phone box between the hall and your house. But from the way he was acting, I think he was checking to see whether anyone was in."

"And were they?"

"Not at the moment."

"Well, that's something, I suppose."

Clare picked up the phone and dialled three nines. When the operator answered, she asked to be put through to the police. Then she explained who she was.

"I need at least two uniforms there and I need you to page Detective Sergeant Dylan and Detective Inspector Greasby."

She looked at her watch. It was two minutes to ten, the worst possible time to call the police.

"What do we do now?" Steve asked.

Really, Clare ought to wait. Dylan would ring her in the next five minutes. They would work out a strategy. But she needed to do something now. And she could speak to Dylan just as easily from Wordsworth Hall as she could from here.

"Can you drive us there?" she asked Sam.

"Straight away."

Should she have rung Neil? Clare wondered, as they sped on to the boulevard. This was his case more than hers. But, no, he was out with his girl-friend, whoever she was. Sam drove into the car park, parking at the steps. While Sam waited in the car, Clare and Steve ran up to the doorway and pressed the buzzer. But the hall's foyer was empty and the door firmly locked. They stood, impotent outside the glass, and waited.

Neil rang Melanie again just before ten, but there was still no reply. Maybe she had the hair-drier on. He couldn't wait any longer, or there wouldn't be time to go out for a drink. It occurred to him for a moment that she had stood him up. Someone had made her a better offer. Would Melanie do that to him? She seemed so warm, so genuine. But he didn't really know her, not yet.

Neil put on his favourite shirt, considered wear-ing a jacket, then rejected the idea because it was still too warm. Melanie was only a five minute walk away. How cold could he get? He was sorry that they hadn't yet got a result over the man who attacked her friends – though Melanie, he had to remind himself, only knew about Lorraine, not Sophie. He hoped that the police's lack of success wouldn't spoil their evening.

Outside, as Neil walked briskly down Hucknall Road, distant police sirens seemed to fill the air, their sound getting steadily nearer. Neil didn't worry. It was Saturday night, when the world and his wife were intent on making trouble. But he, thankfully, was off duty.

Melanie wrapped a towel securely around herself before unlocking the bathroom door. The corridor was empty, which meant that Neil hadn't arrived yet. With her heavy sponge bag in one hand and her door key in the other, she stepped out on to the dull green carpet.

Someone had left the window by the fire escape near her room open, which she hadn't noticed earlier. As a result, the sounds of the city night made the corridor unusually noisy. Beneath the heavy traffic noise, Melanie could make out shouting, sirens and endless dogs barking. On the floor above, someone was playing Bon Jovi, loud. Then, as Melanie put her key in the lock, there was a rattling sound, nearer than all the other noises, followed by a thud.

Melanie tried to open the door quickly but, nervous, she dropped the key. Instead of leaning down to get it, she glanced round to see what the sound was. A man stood there, in a dark T-shirt and blue jeans with the fly open. The ski mask which covered his head had the eyes cut out and his eyes were inhuman, obscene. Melanie froze. He spoke in a gruff, guttural voice.

"Open the door."

In the split second when she had to decide what to do, Melanie thought quickly. He'd meant to push her into the room, the way he had Lorraine. He wouldn't risk attacking her in the corridor, where someone might stumble upon them, and the sound would carry. The masked man took a step towards her, his hand reaching to a pocket. Did he have a weapon? Melanie wasn't waiting around to find out.

"I'm picking up the key," she said, then swung her body round and threw the sponge bag at him. There was an audible thud as his head connected with the heavy glass bottle of scent she kept in the bag. As the man staggered backwards, Melanie ran down the corridor, away from him. She began to shout for help.

"Sorry about that," the porter said. "Had to go to the bathroom." He was talking to Clare, who he recognized. Then he looked at Steve.

"She's not come back yet."

"Is anyone in on C floor?" Clare asked.

"The girl in C3's waiting for someone to arrive."

"Can you tell me the name of the student in B8?" Clare asked. That was the pigeon-hole Steve had seen the rapist looking in.

The porter checked a list.

"Christopher Williams."

"Is he in?"

"I believe so."

Clare calculated. Should she wait? She remembered Chris Williams. He looked so insignificant. What could there possibly be, concealed in his background, to turn him into a violent rapist? Outside, she heard a siren. Suppose he heard it and...

"I'm going upstairs," she told the porter. "Tell the other officers to come up quietly when they arrive."

"Yes, but what's...?"

"Just do as I say."

"I'm coming with you," Steve told her.

"Thanks."

As they climbed the stairs, Clare heard a noise from the floor above.

"Wait outside his door," she told Steve. "I just want to check..." Then someone started to scream. Steve and Clare got to the third floor just as a tall girl in a towel pulled the landing door open. Close behind her, a man in a black ski mask took one look at Clare and Steve, then turned tail.

"It's him," the girl said. "He tried to..."

"It's all right," Clare said, as Steve pushed past her. "We'll get him."

Ruth and Brian were walking into Wordsworth

Hall just as Clare came running down the stairs, followed by a girl wearing nothing but a towel.

"He's on the fire escape!" Clare shouted. "That side!"

She followed Ruth and Brian back into the night and looked around the car park. At first, Clare couldn't see where the fire escape came out. Had he got away already?

The only person around was a young man in shirt sleeves. He walked into the car park with a smile on his face. It was Neil. Before Clare could speak to him, she heard the wallop of a body jumping to the ground, then beginning to run.

"Neil!" she yelled. "Stop him!"

The rapist ran across the car park, pursued by Steve on one side, with Ruth, Clare and Brian on the other. Neil blocked the driveway and the rapist tried to run around him. Neil, who had never played rugby in his life, flung himself at the masked man. He was trying to bring him down in a desperate tackle. Neil half succeeded, knocking the man over, but failing to hang on to him.

It didn't matter. Steve was the next to catch up. He was bigger than both Neil and the rapist. He sat on top of him and pulled off the mask, revealing a spotty, frightened face. Brian helped hold him down while Ruth got out her handcuffs and cuffed him. Only then did Neil look around and see the girl in the towel.

"Melanie!" he said, his voice filled with emotion and fear. "What happened? Did he...?"

She shook her head. "He tried to. I managed to get away."

Clare watched with bewildered feelings as Neil and Melanie embraced.

Next, a car stopped, blocking the driveway, and DS Dylan got out.

"What's going on?"

As Brian and Ruth lifted the rapist to his feet, Clare stepped forward and did the honours.

"Christopher Williams, I'm arresting you for the rapes of Sophie Turner and Lorraine Parker and the attempted rape of Melanie Byatt. You do not have to say anything but..."

"Come on," she half heard Neil saying to Melanie. "Let's get you dressed. We can do the statement in the morning."

Chris Williams had a childlike, pathetic sneer on his face.

"I asked all of them out," he said. "It was their fault, for turning me down. You hear me? I showed those tight..."

"What happened here?" Dylan asked, ignoring the string of obscenities. "Who caught him?"

The four officers looked at each other, no one person wishing to hog the credit. Finally, Clare spoke.

"It was Steve Garrett. He got us here in time and

finished him off, too."

Dylan held out his hand for Steve to shake.

"It looks like you've earned yourself a fresh start," he told him.

By the time DI Greasby arrived, Neil and Melanie were already gone. Greasby got into the car with Ruth and Brian. They took the prisoner into custody. Then Clare turned to Sam, who had been waiting outside during the whole thing. She was standing with Steve.

"Had enough excitement for one night? Ready for the rest of the film?"

Sam shook her head. "I'm going back to Steve's. He wants to talk a few things through. You don't mind…?"

"No," Clare said, not meaning it. "Of course not."

"I'll run you home," Dylan said to her, as Steve got into Sam's car.

"That's good of you, thanks."

During the short drive, Clare filled Chris Dylan in on all of the events of the last half hour.

"Pubs are still open," Dylan said, as they pulled up outside her house. "Fancy a celebratory drink?"

Clare felt shaken up. She didn't want a drink, but she wanted company. She wanted conversation, but not in a crowded pub. She turned to Chris, intending to invite him in for coffee. But then she recognized the look in his eyes. It was the look of a man who thought he was in with a chance. For some men, coming in for coffee always meant something else entirely. Clare didn't want to risk that situation.

"Actually," Clare told Dylan, "I'm dead beat. I think I'll just turn in."

Chris gave her a look which implied that he didn't believe her. Then he said:

"Sleep well, Clare. You did good work tonight."

Clare thanked him and got out of the car. The night was finally turning cool. She let herself into the empty house, switched on all the lights, poured herself a glass of milk, and sat down to watch the rest of the film on her own.

EPILOGUE

Joyce Tate rang the station at twenty to one, just as Ruth and Brian were about to go back on patrol. Ruth took the call.

"It's Roy. He went out at six and hasn't been seen since. I'm worried about what he might do."

Ruth asked a bunch of questions concerning where Roy might have gone, any friends that he could be with, and so on. In the back of her mind, however, she knew where he was.

"We'll find him," she assured Joyce. "We'll try and stop him from doing anything stupid."

"Kimberley's our only grandchild," Joyce told her. "Roy hasn't been sleeping properly since it happened. He cares about her so much. It's driven him crazy."

"We'll do what we can," Ruth promised. She put down the phone and spoke to Brian.

"Roy was in earlier, you said?"

"That's what I heard."

"He'll have seen that?"

She was pointing at the notice giving Ashley Smith's new address.

"Yes."

"I think we'd better get over there."

The flat was in a seedy side-street. Ruth wasn't sure which side of the road it would be on. Then, as they turned into the street, a half-dressed girl ran out of an alley and waved them down.

"What's going on?" Ruth asked.

"Someone smashed the door in. He's beating my friend up!"

"Who's your friend?"

"I don't know his proper name. I met him at Ritzy's, tonight. They call him Smash. Look, what's it matter? I tell you, this guy's killing him!"

Ruth and Brian ran down the alley and up the stairs at the back of a newsagent's. The flat was above the shop. A flimsy door hung loose from its hinges. Ruth kicked it open and ran inside, then followed the sound of screaming.

In a dark, unfurnished room, Roy Tate was on top of Ashley Smith, his fists pummelling the young man's face.

"Roy!" Ruth yelled. "Stop! Roy!"

Her partner turned round, seeing Ruth and Brian.

"Get out and give me two more minutes," he panted. "Then take me in. I haven't finished with this bastard yet."

"Come on," Brian said to Ruth, as Roy resumed the beating. "Let's do what he wants."

"No," Ruth told him. "It's not right."

She and Brian pulled Roy off Smith.

"Don't make us restrain you, Roy," Ruth said. "He's unconscious. You've done enough."

"Enough?" Roy said. "I want him permanently disabled. You think anything but death is enough for, for…"

"That's not for us to say," Ruth told him. "It's over."

Roy's voice was tortured. "It's not over for Kimberley. It'll never be over for Kimberley."

They had him on his feet now. Brian let go and got out his radio.

"Kimberley will learn to live with it," Ruth told Roy. "So will you, in time."

Roy began to cry. Ruth put her arms around him and he rested his head on hers. As they hugged, a cold breeze blew into the room from the open door. Ruth could hear Brian talking over the radio.

"Possible head and chest injuries. His breathing's erratic…"

After a minute or two, Ruth led Roy down to the

car. The girl watching on the street outside was fifteen, at most. She was too scared to look directly at Roy.

"Why did he do it?" she asked. "Smash is a really nice bloke. Why?"

Instead of replying, Ruth got the girl's phone number so that she could call her parents. She told her to wait inside. Then she put Roy in the back of the car and looked at herself in the streetlight. Her white blouse was smeared with Ashley Smith's blood, and she was shivering.

Ruth got out her jacket, put it on. All she wanted to do right now was to go home and curl up in bed, try to sleep. But her shift still had five hours to go.

If you have been the victim of a sexual assault or rape or any other crime, you can ring the following numbers, where someone will be able to help you:

**Victim Support National Helpline:
(0171) 729 1252**

**Childline:
0800 1111**
– the free national helpline for children or young people in trouble or danger.